MW01126435

The Mystery of the Tomahawk Pipe

Jeff Darnell

iUniverse, Inc.
Bloomington

The Mystery of the Tomahawk Pipe

iUniverse books may be ordered through booksellers or by contacting:

iUniverse
1663 Liberty Drive
Bloomington, IN 47403
www.iuniverse.com
1-800-Authors (1-800-288-4677)

ISBN: 978-1-4759-4218-7 (sc)
ISBN: 978-1-4759-4220-0 (hc)
ISBN: 978-1-4759-4219-4 (ebk)

Library of Congress Control Number: 2012914312

Printed in the United States of America

iUniverse rev. date: 09/06/2012

For my parents, Billy Mac and Nancy

Acknowledgments

I would like to express my gratitude to the following people and entities: To Christine Anderson and her mother, Marie Pawlowski, for their time and input. To Judy Baker, Cynthia Ostheimer, and John Baum of the White County Historical Society, for their time, meticulous record keeping, and gracious support. To the Monticello-Union Township Public Library and staff for their assistance. To my dear friends, Kelly Townsend, Varsha Grogan, and Phil Lazarus, for their suggestions and input. To Cathy Morrison, illustrator, for her face-page sketch and kind words. To my wife, Christene, and my children, Shelby and Zach, for their patience and understanding. And to the *Cincinnati Post* and the E.W. Scripps Company for their permission to reprint the article noted in the Prologue.

Prologue

The following article was printed on January 25, 2000, in the *Cincinnati Post.*

"A Haunting Tale of Hidden Gold"

Lester, eighty-five, spends most of his time these days in his bed at a pricey full-care facility on the north side of town. There's something he wants to get off his chest, he says, a family legend he'd like to share while he still has time. The story was handed down to him by his mother, who'd heard it from her father.

Like many similarly intriguing stories, it pushes the bounds of believability. On the other hand, the timing and the circumstances fall within the framework of historical accounts. Stranger things have happened.

In any case, Lester is convinced the story is accurate, as far as it goes. It's been knocking around in his head all his life. He can recall digging for Indian gold himself under an ancient hickory tree on his great-grandfather's Indiana farm when he was a boy.

A central figure in the story is Tecumseh, the great Shawnee chief who organized a huge force of tribes that simultaneously engaged U.S. troops from the shores of the Great Lakes to the banks of the Mississippi, as far east as New York and south to the Gulf shores.

The other central character is Lester's great-grandfather, born around 1807 in White County, Indiana. He was the father of ten children and died at the age of one hundred. Lester describes his great-grandfather this way: "He was a pioneer doctor who studied Indian medicine, raised his own herbs, blended his tonics, and counted among his patients a great many members of the Shawnee nation. As such, he was considered to be a friend to the Shawnee."

Tecumseh's role in history is, of course, well documented. In the 1790s he became one of the leaders of a confederacy of Native Americans dedicated to restoring and preserving their traditional values.

"Within the short space of Tecumseh's life, the Shawnees lost most of their land. They had been driven west from the Scioto to the Great Miami then north into central Ohio toward the Maumee. Now their villages occupied scattered sites in Michigan and the Louisiana Territories and Ohio.

"With their land had gone dreams of reunifying their broken tribe on the Ohio, their ancient home. An inexhaustible tide of white settlement forced upon the Shawnee simple but brutal options. Change and live the settlers' ways or retreat."

Tecumseh eventually allied himself with the British in the War of 1812, helping to ensure the survival of British Canada. He was killed in the Battle of Thames in Ontario in 1813.

Near the end of his life, according to the story that has been handed down in Lester's family, Tecumseh had arranged a shipment of gold, much of it gathered from the tribes in the western regions of the Louisiana Purchase, to Canada.

"His plan was to buy weapons from the British, which he intended to use to prevent the settlers from taking any more Indian land," Lester says.

"He had 4,000 pounds of gold in that shipment. Two hundred stone in all, which would mean it was being transported in 20-pound bars."

The gold, if it existed, never arrived at its destination. Some years after Tecumseh's death in October 1813 at the Battle of Thames in Ontario, Lester says his great-grandfather had occasion to doctor a Shawnee.

"It was this Indian who told (him) about the gold," Lester says.

"He told about how the gold had been carried north on an old Indian trace that ran up through Indiana. Evidently, the Indians who were transporting the gold saw the need to bury it in a hurry, perhaps to keep it from falling into unfriendly hands.

"The way this Shawnee told it, they buried it in White County, on or near his farm."

Lester can still see his father and brothers digging under that old hickory. It was an outstanding landmark, set on high ground. Wherever there was a landmark, Lester says, his father and brothers would sink their shovels in search of Tecumseh's gold.

"My anxiety is for some responsible party to locate that gold and see to it that it's distributed to its rightful owners, whoever the courts decide that may be," Lester says.

"It's just something that ought to happen, something I'd like to see before I die."

Chapter 1

June 6, 1924
Monticello, Indiana

Emmett waited in the dark of the night and then finally whispered, "Mackie!" He waited a few moments more, peered around the corner of the shed, cupped his hands, and in a louder whisper called again. "Mackie! Come on." He pulled back around the corner, sat on the ground, and waited.

"I'm comin'," a voice answered from across the way. A few seconds later, a short, stout boy shuffled through the tall grass and plopped down next to Emmett behind the shed. Billy Mac was huffing and puffing, so Emmett let the younger boy catch his breath.

The ground was cool, and Emmett could feel the damp through his dungarees.

"We probably don't have to be so skittish," he said. "There's no moon. It's dark back here in the trees. He probably can't see us from inside the house."

"Don't hurt to be careful," Billy Mac mumbled.

Emmett bent forward, knee-walked to his corner of the shed, and looked at the house. It was all lit up and easy enough to see a man walk from room to room carrying boxes.

"What're you thinkin' of doing, Emmo?" Billy Mac asked. He sounded a little nervous.

"Don't know, Mackie. Maybe nothing. Just looking. You all right?"

"Look, Emmo," Billy Mac said, "I know you're sore at Skinner for what happened to Maddie."

"So?" Emmett countered without turning around.

"So he just didn't know nobody," Billy Mac argued. "He'd just got to town—barely made it to the new schoolhouse in time for the dedication and social. He was just tryin' to make polite conversation. I don't think he meant to embarrass her in front of everyone."

Emmett didn't answer. He studied Skinner's house, watching the new resident.

"Look," Billy Mac said, "he's gonna be the principal when the schoolhouse opens in the fall. I just don't think we should be stalkin' him! Besides, you ever seen Maddie when she couldn't take care of herself?"

Emmett didn't answer again but turned and looked at Billy Mac. Billy Mac sat there, a frown on his face, kicking at a pile of sawdust. Emmett grinned to himself.

The truth was, in his sixteen years, Emmett Trentham couldn't remember a time in his life when Billy Mac Finch had not been around. Neither had brothers or sisters, and they had simply gravitated toward each other at some young age. Emmett's natural love of books and curiosity made schooling easy for him, so through the years he had often helped the slightly younger boy, who struggled with his studies. He knew Billy Mac accepted him as the unspoken leader of the two. He often laughed and poked fun at Billy Mac's more solemn demeanor.

"He must've just had this shed built," Billy Mac mumbled, still kicking at a pile of sawdust.

Emmett shook his head, amused at Billy Mac's cautious nature, and then turned back to study the house.

"Hey, Emmo! This ain't a shed. It's an outhouse—look!"

Emmett turned around. "Huh? What?" he asked. He edged back over and sat down.

Billy Mac held up a piece of scrap wood he had picked out of the sawdust. He handed it to Emmett. It was shaped like a crescent moon.

Emmett looked at Billy Mac and moved his eyebrows up and down a few times. "It sure is," he said. "Well, what do you know? A new outhouse."

"What're you thinkin,' Emmo?"

"Skinner moved to town a few days ago, right?" Emmett said. "He doesn't know the yard out here that well yet. Especially if he just had this baby built." He patted the wall of the outhouse. "It's not settled into the ground yet. Should be easy to move. We're going to just scoot it back a few feet," he said with a smile.

"We can't do that," Billy Mac said. "What if he falls in?"

"So what if he does?" Emmett replied. "It's a brand new pit. There's nothing down this hole that's going to hurt him. It's not been used enough—maybe not used at all yet." He scooted back to the corner and looked at the house. Skinner was still sorting boxes.

After a minute, Emmett went back and sat down. Billy Mac still had a frown on his face.

"Look, Mackie," he began, "remember last year when I was sick and missed so much school? I sat by that window in my bedroom and read everything Ms. Lee would send over from the library. Well, there was a new book about a fat little bear that ate honey all the time. He had this rabbit friend that lived in a tree. One day the bear is visiting the rabbit inside the tree and eats so much honey that when he goes to leave he gets stuck crawling through the hole to get out. Skinner's the same way. He's so fat that he won't fall into the privy pit. At worst, he'll just get stuck." He smiled to himself. "Wouldn't that be a sight!"

Billy Mac sighed. "I don't know."

"Come on, Mackie. We're not tearing anything up." Emmett continued. "We're just moving something. Skinner will blame the workers for not putting the privy over the hole when they finished."

"Okay, okay," Billy Mac said. "Wanna do it tonight or tomorrow night?"

"Well, where's your pa tonight, at home or down at the jailhouse?" Emmett asked.

"Jailhouse," Billy Mac answered. "Won't be home for a while since it's Friday night. He's got late rounds to make. Is your ma home?"

Emmett looked through the trees and across the street to the far corner. It was pitch black. "Doesn't look like it. She's still at the Strand. Some singing group's coming through. She heard them on that new tube radio she bought for the theater. Went down early to make sure everything is set up right. She'll stay until it's over with." He turned back to study the house. "They got a guy named Bing that's really supposed to be something. Why would you give a kid a name like that?"

"I don't know," Billy Mac mumbled. "Look, if we're gonna do this, let's do it. You get that corner, and I'll take this one. We'll try to pull it back."

Several minutes and twelve inches later, Emmett plopped back on the ground; Billy Mac did the same beside him.

"Dang thing's heavier than it looks," Emmett puffed between breaths. "Criminy!"

He stretched out on the ground. The cool earth felt good. The crickets were getting loud.

"Wonder why Skinner moved up here to start with?" Billy Mac asked. "Why didn't he just stay in Lafayette?"

Emmett sat up. "'To foster the broadening of young horizons and to ameliorate the milieu and curriculum allowing them to do so,' according to Mr. Bausman down at the *Herald*. He interviewed Skinner last week." He looked at Billy Mac and smiled.

Billy Mac shook his head at Emmett. "How do you know all this stuff, Emmo? You know more about everything than anybody I ever met."

"I read." Emmett shrugged.

He stood up and peeked at the house. "Okay, let's finish this. I don't see Skinner moving around in there anymore. Let's get around in front and see if we can push it easier than pulling it."

Crouching low, each took a front corner.

"Wait a minute," Billy Mac said. He took his cap off, threw it on the ground, and wiped his forehead. "Okay."

"I'll push my side first," Emmett whispered. "Then you do your side and we'll work it back and forth. Here we go—umph!"

"It's movin'. It's movin'," Billy Mac grunted.

"Keep going," Emmett said. "Just a little further . . . a little more . . . a little more . . . keep going. That's it! Hold it right there. Wow! Would you look at that?!"

In the dark of night, the pit was just a two-foot-wide black spot on the ground. The door of the outhouse was a few long steps beyond.

"C'mon. Let's sit down for a minute," Emmett said, and he walked back behind the privy.

Billy Mac followed and sat next to him. He picked up the wooden moon. "Okay, so tell me this: Why do they cut holes shaped like moons in outhouses?"

"The short version," Emmett replied with a smile, "is that you have to have a hole for fresh air and light. In the old days when most people couldn't read, the holes for male privies were star-shaped and holes for female privies had moon shapes—so they could tell 'his' and 'hers' apart. I guess most men didn't bother making the trip to the john; they'd just go behind a tree. After a while they stopped making separate privies for men. So now they all just have a moon."

Billy Mac just shook his head.

Emmett smiled. "I read it in *Popular Mechanics*. Come on. Let's get out of here."

Emmett led the way as they walked through the trees, careful to stay in the shadows.

"Wait, I gotta get my hat," Billy Mac said behind him.

Emmett turned and saw the boy trot back to the outhouse. He followed, and as he slipped around the corner of the outhouse, he watched Bill Mac step into the dark circle of the pit and disappear with a cry.

"Aaarrrggghhh!"

"What the—oh, rats!" Emmett whispered as he ran up. "Be quiet. Be still." He crouched down next to the hole.

A dog barked in the distance. After a minute it quit and all Emmett could hear was crickets.

"Mackie, you okay?" Emmett whispered down into the hole.

"Yeah," Billy Mack whispered back. "Scraped up a bit. My nose is bleedin'. I'm gonna kill you when I get out, Emmo!"

"Rats!" Emmett cried. "I can't believe you fell in!" Then he added, "How deep is it? Hold your hands up."

Two hands stuck up out of the ground.

"Emmo, this pit is not completely unused," Billy Mac groaned. "Get me out of here! Now!"

"Okay, okay," Emmett replied. He straddled the hole, one foot on each side, and reached down to grab Billy Mac's hands. "He had all those workers in and out of the house for all those days. I guess it must have been them that used it. Okay, on three, you jump and I'll pull so you can get up on the edge and work your way out. One . . . two . . . three! Humph!" He grunted as he pulled Billy Mac up.

Billy Mac crawled out, rolled over, and lay on his back. He pinched his nose together.

"Still bleeding?" Emmett asked. He crouched down beside the younger boy. "How bad is it?"

"Gnot du mush, I tink," Billy Mac mumbled. "Lemme lay 'ere fur a mint."

Emmett sat quietly for a minute and then said, "You sure are scraped up. We've got to do something about your clothes and . . . oh, rats! Where's your other shoe?!"

Billy Mac sat up and felt around on the ground. "I don't know. Gotta be here somewhere, or else—Emmo! I ain't going back down there!" he whispered.

"You have to, Mackie. You can't let Skinner find your shoe down there."

"I ain't going back down there, Emmo!"

"There's no other way to get it. We can't fish it out with a stick. You can't see the bottom from up here. You've got to."

"I ain't going back down there. I just ain't!"

A dog barked again in the distance. Finally, Emmett said, "Okay, Mackie, okay. The only thing we can do is push the privy back to where it was and then throw some leaves down there to cover it up. Then we'll go down to the creek and get you and your clothes cleaned up a little. You'll have to hide them someplace until they dry and you can sneak 'em into wash day." He stood up. "C'mon."

"I'm gonna kill you, Emmo," Billy Mac growled as he dragged himself to his feet.

The boys walked home from the creek. They'd tossed the other shoe into the creek and scrubbed the muck off of Billy Mac. Emmett grinned as he watched the boy gingerly walk on the gravel in his bare feet. Billy Mac looked like an unhappy drowned rat.

They crept through the alley to Billy Mac's back porch. Billy Mac went up the steps, and just as he opened the screen door to go in, Emmett asked, "Mackie, you have your hat?"

"Yes, Emmo, I got my stupid hat. Just shut up."

Emmett paused and then asked, "Wonder what we can do to Skinner now to make up for Maddie?"

Billy Mac looked at him, waved him off, and turned to go in. "Leave it alone, Emmo. Just leave it be." He went in and quietly closed the door behind him.

Emmett stood there for a minute and then chuckled as he turned back to the alley. *What a night!*

Chapter 2

Billy Mac reached under the hen, slowly pulled out a brown egg, and put it in his bucket. *Okay, just eight more.* He took a few steps, bent over—winced—and reached under another hen. It hurt to stretch. His fall into the pit the night before had bruised him up. He thought about the night before. *Wonder where Emmo is? He shoulda been 'round by now. He couldn't be in trouble with Skinner or else I'da been called out, too. I'll find him after I drop these eggs off.*

Billy Mac finished gathering the eggs, picked up the first bucket he had already filled, and carried them both out of the hen house through the fence gate and across the yard. He walked into the house and put both buckets on the kitchen counter and then pumped water to fill each. He filled a third, empty bucket too. After the eggs soaked, he rubbed them one by one, cleaning the fluff and debris off them. Then he dipped each egg into the bucket of clean water to rinse them. He dried each with a wash rag and lit a candle. One by one he passed each egg across the front of the flame. The candlelight created a soft glow through the translucent shells. Billy Mac looked at each egg for hairline cracks. Finding none, he put them in twelve-count boxes. *Perfect. With those from yesterday, that's twelve dozen eggs. Mr. Morris will be happy to have these.*

He carried in some stove wood and corncobs, stacked them in the box, checked the kerosene levels in the lanterns, got the eggs from the day before out of the ice box, and checked to see if a new block of ice was needed. Billy Mac then went to the table, picked up his sketch pad, looked at the outhouse he had drawn on it, and shook his head. *I'm gonna kill Emmo.*

Billy Mac secretly wished he could be more like his friend—taller and thinner, well-kept instead of his own disheveled appearance. Emmett could talk properly, and people just naturally liked him. He was easygoing and quick to laugh. Billy Mac had only seen him angry a few times; Emmett's good nature could turn on a dime in the face of blatant injustice. A stray dog or cat that unwittingly wound up in the clutches of a prankster would find a resolute ally in Emmett.

Billy Mac closed the sketch pad, put it and his pencils into his backpack, slung it onto his back, and then picked up the eggs to take to Morris's Market.

He pushed the screen door out with his backside, let the spring pop it back—catching it with his foot so it didn't slam too hard—turned, walked down the porch steps, and then walked along the bluff towards town and Morris's. He looked down at the Tippecanoe River. *No boats. Quiet down there today.*

As he approached the new school building on his right, he stopped in the dirt road and glanced across the street at the Skinners' house. He looked to the backyard and then out into the trees at the back of the lot. The new outhouse was sitting pretty as could be with the crescent moon on the front door as if it were mocking him. Billy Mac shook his head and the thought of being in the pit riled him, again.

"Hey, Mackie!" The voice startled Billy Mac back to the present, and he almost dropped his twelve cartons of eggs. He looked around but didn't see anyone.

"Hey, Mackie! Up here!"

Billy Mac looked up and there was Emmett grinning and waving to him from Principal Skinner's second-floor window.

Oh, no! What's he done, now? "Emmo! What're you doin' up there?" Billy Mac shouted. "Jeezus! Did you do somethin' to—"

"No, no." Emmett smiled and waved his hands back and forth. "Everything's fine. Look, meet me at the front door."

Billy Mac walked up the steps. The door opened and there stood Emmett with a smile on his face. "C'mon in. No one's here."

"Emmo, you can't be goin' into Skinner's house when he's not—," Billy Mac started.

"It's okay. I'm supposed to be in here." Emmett cut him off. "C'mon. Come in so I can close the door." He ushered Billy Mac in.

"Wow! He's sure got a lot of stuff, don't he?" Billy Mac commented, looking around at all the boxes that hadn't been unpacked yet. He walked around and looked down the hall. "Man, look at all the plaster work. What a place! This has got to be one of the nicest places in town."

"Yeah," Emmett replied. "Ma volunteered me to help him; she said we should be making some extra money. Now that the first dam is done and we're finally going to get some electricity, she wants to buy some of those new gizmos I've read about. She wants one of those floor sweepers and an electric iron. And a radio like she has down at the Strand so she can listen at night from home. Ackerman's Music Shop has them now."

"I know," Billy Mac said. "Pa wants a 'lectric ice box. And some 'lectric lights so he can read better. Drives him nuts to have 'em down at the jailhouse and not at home." *These lights they got in here sure are nice.* He reached over and flicked a switch a few times.

"Anyway," Emmett said, "I've been unpacking stuff and moving and cleaning stuff and sweeping. You name it, I'm doing it."

"And you ain't done nothin' to get back at him for Maddie?" Billy Mac asked. He squinted at Emmett, daring him to tell him the truth. "When I saw you in that window I thought you'd flipped and done somethin' *really* stupid."

Emmett mocked surprise. "Me? Nooo!" They both laughed.

"You know what?" Emmett said. "He's really not that bad of a guy. We got on pretty good. I'm over the Maddie thing, but I did tell him that he really embarrassed her. You know what he said? 'I did not have in mind an unseemly affect and, not being acquainted with Ms. Miller, was ignorant of her shy comportment. Though innocent in my intent, I would be grateful if you would convey to her my regrets, for I fear my direct profession would result in repeat mortification.'" The boys laughed again.

Billy Mac said, "I'm glad you get it 'cause I sure don't. So where is he?"

"Gone to Lafayette to get his wife," Emmett answered. "Guess he got married a few weeks ago. That's why he's been working so hard to get this place settled. He's even going to have the outside repainted next week. I guess the new Mrs. Skinner has a thing for green. She wants a green house." Emmett nodded at the egg cartons. "You taking those to Morris's?" he asked.

"Yeah," Billy Mac answered. "You stuck in here all day?"

"Yep." Then Emmett said, "Hey, Mackie, you've got to see this before you go. Skinner had something else done in here too. You'll probably never be in here, again, right? Follow me."

Emmett turned and started up the staircase. Billy Mac followed. Half way down a hall Emmett turned in through a door. Billy Mac followed him into a small room, and Emmett stood there grinning, hands on his hips.

"Would you look at that?" he asked, nodding into one of the corners.

"Wow! I ain't never seen one!" Billy Mac exclaimed. There, in a room covered with new white tiling on the floor and walls, was a white wash tub and sink, each with their own running water, and a white indoor toilet. "It's the whitest room I've ever seen. Jeez!"

"Sure is a sight, isn't it?" Emmett said.

"What'dya think he had that new privy built out back for with this in here?" Billy Mac asked.

"I'll bet this is for his new wife," Emmett answered. "I bet he still goes out back. Some people are just funny that way—it's hard to break old habits. I sure hope she's happy after all the things he's had done. When she sees this, it ought to do the trick," he said with a laugh.

"Emmo," Billy Mac asked, "have you worked that john, yet?"

"Yeah," Emmett answered. "A few times. You just push down on the handle. Here, watch."

Emmett pushed the handle and Billy Mac watched the whirlpool suck all the water out and then slowly fill up.

"Do you think it gets clogged up easy?" Billy Mac asked. "That hole looks awful small."

"It's supposed to work great," Emmett said. "Hey . . . ," he started.

Billy Mac looked at him. Emmett smiled and twitched his eyebrows up and down a few times. His eyes were sparkling. "Wanna try it?" he asked.

"No, way! There's no way I'm gonna sit on there and—"

"No, not that!" Emmett said. "Let's try it with something else. Hand me a carton of those eggs."

"We can't do that. Pa'd kill me," Billy Mac protested.

"Morris is not going to miss a few eggs," Emmett argued. "He doesn't know how many you're bringing does he?"

"No, I guess not," Billy Mac mumbled. He handed Emmett a carton. "He only pays for what I bring."

"Okay, watch this. One, two, three . . . flush!" Emmett dropped the egg into the middle of the whirlpool and it disappeared straight through the hole. "Whoa!"

"It didn't even touch the sides—just went straight through!" Billy Mac said. "Lemme try." He was caught up in it now and grabbed two eggs. "Two at once. One, two, three . . . flush!"

Emmett and Billy Mac took turns. Two eggs turned into three at once and then four and five and six. Before they knew it, twelve dozen eggs were gone.

"Whattaya mean the eggs're gone?" Billy Mac's face turned white. "They can't be all gone," he groaned.

Emmett shrugged. "They are," he replied.

"Oh, Emmo! I've gotta take eggs to the Morris's," Billy Mac said. "They gotta have 'em for the market. Oh, Emmo! What'm I gonna do? It took me three days to gather all them eggs. I've already cleaned out both hen houses."

"I don't know, Mackie. Swear I don't. Rats!"

Billy Mac sat on the floor. He felt sick to his stomach. "Nothing I can do 'cept tell Pa I used 'em all. I can't lie to him. Oh, Emmo, twelve dozen eggs!"

Billy Mac sat on the front porch swing waiting. *What if Mr. Morris won't buy eggs from us anymore? Jeezus! Here comes Pa.* He looked down at his feet to study the knot hole he was kicking at.

"Son?"

"Yes, Pa?"

"Mr. Morris says he didn't get eggs today."

"No, sir."

"Want to tell me why?"

Billy Mac looked up at him. "It's my fault, Pa. I . . . I lost 'em." He grimaced. "I'd rather not say how."

"How many did you lose?"

"Twelve dozen."

"You lost a hundred and forty-four eggs and you'd rather not say how?"

"No, sir."

Seconds ticked by that felt like an eternity. "Was Emmett involved?"

"Yes, sir. But it was my fault."

"I see. You won't be getting any allowance until those eggs are paid for. Understand?"

"Yes, sir."

"I told Mr. Morris it will not happen, again. Will it?"

"No, sir."

"And, after supper tonight, you'll go see Mr. Morris and assure him of that fact yourself, right?"

"Yes, sir."

His father went through the screen door and it popped closed on the spring with a clap. Billy Mac shook his head. *Jeezus, Emmo. A hundred an' forty-four eggs.*

Chapter 3

The boys lay on top of sleeping bags on Emmett's back porch. Billy Mac listened to the crickets and looked up at the clear sky. The sliver of a new moon was already high. *My favorite time of the year.*

"Hey, Emmo," he said, "Lookit that. That's the first lightnin' bug I seen this year. Look."

"I see it," Emmett answered. "So, Mackie, about the other day, you didn't get a whipping or nothing?"

"No. I'm too old for a whippin', and I think he knew I was feelin' bad enough already," Billy Mac said. *A falling star! I wish . . . I wish the wind would blow. Jeez, it's hot.* "He asked me if you was involved."

"Really?" Emmett asked. "And?"

"Jeez, Emmo, I can't lie to him. I told him you was there," Billy Mac said. "I didn't tell him what we did, just said it was my fault." Then he added, "It was different. Not like when I was little. More like we could kinda talk about it. He wasn't that sore. It was okay." Billy Mac closed his eyes.

"Huh," Emmett grunted. "Hey, I've got something for you, Mackie. Ma was listening to her radio down at the Strand before she came home tonight. Said there's this new show in Tennessee called the country opera barn dance or something. Had their first broadcast tonight. Well, after the show there was this news update and there's a guy named Shipwreck Kelly out

East that's got everyone worked up about sitting on flagpoles. Can you believe it?"

"He sits on flagpoles?" Billy Mac asked.

"Yeah. He climbs to the top of a flagpole and sits on it," said Emmett. "He sat on the top of a flag pole for thirteen hours straight, and now people all over are doing it. They're going nuts. Bunches of them, all over the place, sitting on flagpoles."

"His name's Shipwreck?" Billy Mac asked.

"That's what the radio said," answered Emmett. "Said he'd survived the Titanic when he was a kid. Now he's grown up and goes by the name Shipwreck. Can't blame a guy for that, I guess."

"What's he climbin' and sittin' on the top of flagpoles for?" asked Billy Mac.

"I guess because it hasn't been done before," said Emmett. "According to him, he's going to set all sorts of records and make a bunch of money. Shoot, wouldn't be hard to set a record for something no one's done before, would it?"

"I guess not," said Billy Mac. Then, realization hit. *Uh-oh.* He opened his eyes and sat up. "What'dya thinkin', Emmo?"

"I'm thinking we need to do something around here that no one else has done before," Emmett answered. "Something different. Just to be able to say we had done it."

Billy Mac shrugged. *Not a bad idea.* "Well, we can't do flagpoles—that's already being done." He lay back down, looked at the sky, and listened to the crickets.

"I know!" Emmett said. "We'll sneak over to the livery in the middle of the night . . ."

"Oh, no," Billy Mac groaned. *Not another night thing. I'm still skinned up from the last one.*

"And take a wagon apart," Emmett continued. "We'll take the pieces and put them back together in the middle of the new schoolhouse. No one's ever done anything like that around here before!"

Billy Mac smiled. *That is good. Imagine workers goin' in to finish up inside the new schoolhouse and findin' a wagon. Jeez!*

"Wouldn't be a bad idea," Billy Mac replied, "if we knew how to take a wagon apart, if we had a place to do it, and if we had the tools. Besides, that would be stolen property. Don't think Pa would be too keen on that."

"Yeah," Emmett conceded, "you're right. Hmph!"

Neither boy spoke for a minute. The silence was broken by the distant whistle of a train as it rolled through town.

"Hey, Emmo," said Billy Mac, "let's try something a little easier to start with and work our way up. I'll bet with a little practice we can walk for miles on a train track without falling off. There has to be a record in that, somehow."

"Mackie, good man!" Emmett stood up and put both arms out. "I've got great balance."

Billy Mac could see Emmett's black silhouette wobbling back and forth as he put one step in front of the other on his imaginary train track.

"And," Emmett continued, "if we go east, across the bridge, we just might see Maddie."

Billy Mac shook his head. *So that's it. Good grief.*

"Yeah, right," Billy Mac mumbled and rolled over. "Night, Emmo."

Chapter 4

"Rats!" Emmett swore.

Billy Mac stopped, held his arms out for balance, looked over at Emmett, and smiled. *Your eight to my one. This is great!*

"You're tryin' too hard," Billy Mac said. "You gotta just feel it, and you can't look down right at your feet. Gotta kinda look up ahead a little bit." He started forward on his rail again, arms straight out.

"Look, Mackie," Emmett said, "you do it your way and I'll do it mine. I can balance just fine. Dew's just not lifted over here yet. Your side is in the sun. Mine's still in the shade—it's wet and slippery."

"Wanna trade sides?" Billy Mac asked, eyes straight ahead.

"No, I don't wanna trade sides!" Emmett scolded.

Hmph. Gettin' mad. That sure don't happen too often. How funny! "Fine. See ya 'round," Billy Mac said. He moved ahead at a good pace.

Billy Mac walked on in silence. *Morning sunshine sure feels good.* He stopped, balanced, and closed his eyes. *Smells good out of town, too. Sun burning off the wet of the night: honeysuckle, grapevine, Queen Anne's Lace. Nice and quiet. Wonder what it'd be like bein' a hobo and ridin' the rails and . . .*

"Rats! I'm gonna . . ." Emmett's rant startled Billy Mac and he lost his balance too, falling off his rail into the gravel of the track bed.

"Look, Emmo, let's take a break and just walk a bit," Billy Mac said.

"Yeah, okay," Emmett mumbled. "Come on."

"How far you think we've come?" Billy Mac asked. He picked up a rock and threw it at a tree stump in the distance. *Missed.*

"Maybe a mile or so," Emmett said.

"A mile? I walked a mile and only fell off once?" Billy Mac teased. He shot a side glance at Emmett. "Reckon that's a record?"

Emmett stopped, put his hands on his hips, and glared back at Billy Mac. Finally he smiled and nodded. "Yeah, Mackie, I reckon that's a record. Good man. Come on." And he started walking again. "We're probably getting pretty close to the Millers' farm."

"Think Maddie's around?" Billy Mac asked. *I wish he'd just fess up to how much he likes her. Drives me nuts.*

"Well, they usually go to town on Saturday for the market," Emmett said. "Never know though. Maybe we can stop by the farm for a drink of water."

"Shoulda brought some with us," Billy Mac said. "Wasn't thinkin' or I'da stuck a canteen in my backpack and—hey! Lookit that!" He pointed to an old log cabin off in the scrub. Vines and brush hid all but the upper half. Most of the roof had fallen in leaving a skeletal cage of beams.

"Whoa! Let's check it out," Emmett said.

Billy Mac watched Emmett scamper down off of the track bed and into the undergrowth.

"Come on," Emmett called.

Reluctantly Billy Mac followed Emmett's trail through the brush. Small, tender green grasshoppers skirted out in front of his boots.

When Billy Mac caught up, Emmett was standing in front of what was once the front porch.

"Careful," Emmett said. "Don't put your weight on the middle of the boards—might fall through. Walk along the edges where there's support."

Billy Mac inched along the edge behind Emmett, testing his footing with each step until they'd worked around and got through the front door.

"Jeez," Billy Mack said. "Just a dirt floor." He walked around investigating. *Wouldn't that be a strange way to live?* "Not much in here." He walked over to the fireplace. Bricks were missing out of the corners. "Look here. These bricks are so old they're soft." He pulled one out. Right away a few above it fell out too, and he jumped back.

"Whoa!" Emmett exclaimed. "Look out, Mackie! You'll pull the whole thing down on top of us."

"Yeah," Billy Mac answered and turned toward the door. "Let's get out of here. Nothing in here anyway, and . . . Emmo, what're you doin'?"

Emmett stood, staring at the fireplace. He bent down and picked up a couple of bricks, turned toward Billy Mac, and smiled.

"Bet I can bring the whole thing down with three throws," he said. He weighed a brick up and down in his hand. "What do you think?"

"I think you're nuts," countered Billy Mac. "If that thing falls on us, nobody will ever know what happened to us." He eyed the fireplace. *That chimney's probably twenty feet tall. Bet it'll take at least six throws anyway.*

Emmett nodded at some bricks on the ground by Billy Mac's feet. "I'll let you go first," he said with a smile.

"Okay, but here's the deal," Billy Mac said. "On each throw we both light out runnin' for shelter 'cause if it comes down, it's comin' straight across the floor here. I head for the front door; you head out the back. No takin' chances. Deal?"

"Deal," agreed Emmett and took a few steps toward the back door. "Take your best shot."

Billy Mac took his backpack off and put it on the ground by the front door. He walked back to the center of the room, picked up a brick, took aim, and hurled it. The brick hit to the right of the hearth opening. Five or six bricks easily broke away.

"Nice one!" said Emmett. "Here I go." He flung a brick at the left of the opening. Several more bricks fell.

They took turns whittling away at the base of the structure.

"Look, we gotta aim up higher, toward the narrow part of the chimney." Billy Mac pointed. "We'll never bring it down by hitting down low where it's so big. Watch." His throw took out enough bricks to make the chimney shudder. Both boys scrambled for safety.

Nothing happened. Billy Mac eased his way back into the room. He saw Emmett doing the same on the far side of the cabin.

"Good shot, Mackie!" Emmett called. "Now watch this."

Emmett eyed his target, launched his brick, and knocked out the whole front side of the chimney chute. The tower of bricks wobbled forward and then back, and then it broke forward with a rush, crashing across the remains of the roof beams and driving down into the dirt floor with a splintering thunder. Dirt plumes shot up, engulfing the whole cabin in a thick cloud of gray.

The silence following the crash was complete.

Billy Mac stood in the doorway waiting for the rubble and dirt to settle. He looked around the room and then saw it. Outside of a window opening at the end of the cabin he saw what looked to be a person standing there. Startled, he blinked the dust out of his eyes and waved the dirt cloud away from his face and looked again. This time he saw nothing.

"Mackie!" Emmett's voice called through the dirt cloud.

"Yeah?" Billy Mac called back, still looking around for a person.

"You okay?"

"Yeah." Billy Mac turned his attention back to the roof that caved in. "Jeezus, Emmo. You all right?"

"I'm good. Whoa! What a crash, huh?"

"Did you see that?" Billy Mac called through the cloud of dirt.

"Of course I saw it," Emmett yelled back. "Biggest crash I ever made!"

"Not the crash," Billy Mac said. "That person. Right after the crash I saw someone standin' in that window space at the end of the cabin. You didn't see it?"

"Nope. I couldn't see anything through that cloud of dirt. You're seeing things, Mackie," Emmett yelled. "Meet me inside."

Billy Mac made his way back inside the cabin, waving the dust out of his face. He found Emmett standing in front of the hearth.

"Whoa!" Emmett said. "Would you look at that?"

Billy Mac followed Emmett's gaze. The brick pile lay all the way from the hearth across the floor to the far end of the cabin, in much the same shape as the chimney had been. Broken ceiling beams lay scattered.

"Pretty impressive, huh?" Emmett chuckled.

"Yeah. Pretty impressive," Billy Mac answered. *How does he talk me into these things?* "You lost your bet. It took more than three throws."

Emmett walked to the hearth and poked his head into the opening. "Not technically," he said. "Once we threw up at the chimney part it only took two." He pulled some loose bricks down out of the inside of the hearth. "Hey, Mackie! There's something in here."

"What?" Billy Mac asked. "Somethin' in where?"

"Not sure. It's dark on the other side of this hole in here—no sunlight," Emmett said. He picked up a few chunks, hit the wall a couple times to make the gap bigger, and then reached up and pulled a section of bricks and mortar down. "Whoa! There's a little room back there!"

"What'dya mean a room?" Billy Mac asked and moved in closer.

"I mean a little room," Emmett answered. "It's like a closet space. I think I see some shelves and stuff. I'm squeezing through."

"Wait, Emmo," warned Billy Mac. "Wait a minute, and . . ." Emmett was gone. There was nothing but a dark hole where he'd been standing. *Jeez!*

Chapter 5

"Come on, squeeze through," Emmett called through the hole. "There's plenty of room."

Billy Mac looked around, still uneasy about the person he thought he'd seen. He made sure no one was watching, picked up his backpack, and walked to the opening. He turned sideways, stepped up high to fit one leg through, found the floor on the other side, and then slid through, balancing on one foot as he inched inside. "Dark in here," he murmured.

"It's not bad after you get used to it," Emmett said. "Just stand there for a minute." Billy Mac could hear Emmett shuffling around.

"Still can't see real good with that big piece of chimney covering the hole up there," Emmett said. "Hey! I've got an idea."

Emmett picked up a brick and started tapping softly on the outside wall at about eye level. "I'll knock a brick or two out and make a window, let some light in." The brick in the wall easily gave way and a sharp beam of light shot through the gray, dusty air. "Perfect. Here, I'll do a few more."

Billy Mac's eyes adjusted and he moved around to look at the stuff on one of the shelves. He waved his hand back and forth, blowing off a layer of grime and cobwebs. He could see an old bird nest in one corner. There was a small stack of candles and some old kitchen matches, long past their days of use. “Smells like an old root cellar that’s been closed up too long,” he said.

“Yeah,” Emmett agreed. “Hey! Look at this.” He picked up a small, flat, square piece of metal, blew on it, and sneezed from the dust. Then he wiped it with his shirt sleeve.

“It’s a picture,” Emmett said. “Of a girl—no, a woman.” He carried it over to one of the holes he had made in the brick wall and held the picture frame up into the light streaming through.

“Whoa! It’s Maddie!” he exclaimed. “No. It can’t be; this is an old picture.” He squinted and looked a little closer.

“Lemme see,” Billy Mac said. He walked over, took the picture, and moved into the light so he could see it better. *Wow! It does look like her, except for the old-time dress. Small face, dark hair, dark eyes, bangs hanging down, head tilted, pretty smile . . . just like Maddie.* “You know, we’re probably on Miller property by now. Maddie’s grandpa has lived on that farm for a long time. Maybe his family lived in this cabin way back when.” He shrugged.

“Sure is a spittin’ image,” Emmett said. He took the picture back from Billy Mac, studied it, and put it in his pocket.

A dog barked and a voice trailed behind it. Billy Mac could hear something scrubbing through the bushes outside the cabin and then a soft thump as something jumped through the door.

“I told you there was someone out there!” Billy Mac hissed.

“Wait a minute, boy!” a voice called after the dog. Something shuffled closer to the front of the fireplace, and Billy Mac could hear the sniffing of a dog on the trail. A few seconds later, a golden retriever stuck his face through the opening, sniffing nose and all.

Boomer! Billy Mac smiled, reached over, and rubbed between the dog’s ears.

Then, right above Boomer's head, Maddie Miller peeked through, waving the dust out of her way. She squinted and her puzzlement gave way to a smile.

"Hey, guys," she said, shaking her head. "Why am I not surprised?"

"Hey, Maddie," Billy Mac and Emmett echoed.

She tilted her head, just a little, to let her bangs fall from her eyes.

Chapter 6

Billy Mac helped Maddie crawl through the hole.

"I was sitting on the other side of the creek when I heard the crash." She picked up a few things from a shelf, looked at them, and put them down.

"This cabin belongs to your family, Maddie?" Emmett asked.

"Sure does," she answered. "Gramps was born here. Showed it to me for the first time when I was a little girl."

"Maddie, did you see anyone else out there 'round the cabin?" Billy Mac asked.

Maddie looked surprised. "No. Why?"

"Aw, get off it, Mackie," Emmett said. He turned to Maddie and waved a hand toward Billy Mac. "He's seeing things." Then he added, "What's this hidden room doing back here?"

"Gramps always told stories about how folks had secret spaces behind their fireplaces," Maddie said. "So they could hide. Said they hid a few times when Indians came poking around, back when he was a boy."

"So your great-grampa was here first," Emmett mused. He bent down to see what Boomer was pawing at in the corner.

"Yeah," Maddie answered. She stood on her tiptoes to look up on the shelf. "He was a doctor, too, just like Gramps. It's been a long, long time since anyone's lived out here. Gramps built our farmhouse when he and Grandma first got married." She swept the dust from a shelf with her hand.

Billy Mac walked over. "Anything up there, Maddie?" He stretched his hand up and to the back of a shelf and felt something. He got hold of an object and pulled it down to look at it. "What is . . . hey, a hatchet!"

Maddie edged closer. "No, it's not," Maddie said. She took it from his hands and walked over to a stream of light. "It's a tomahawk. Look at it!" She rubbed the leather bindings that held the cutting stone in place and then felt down the wooden handle. "Look at all the carvings in the handle."

"No," said Emmett leaning over. "It's more. Here, let me see."

Emmett turned it so that the cutting edge of the tomahawk pointed toward the ground. The side sticking up had a little cup fitting to it. "Look," he pointed. "It's a pipe. I've read about them." He shook his head back and forth. "These were special. They were used for rituals and stuff, important occasions. Like a peace pipe."

Emmett reached up and felt along the shelf where Billy Mac had found the tomahawk pipe. He pulled down a dirty sheet of paper. "What's this?" He blew a layer of dust off of it and held it in the light so he could see it better.

Billy Mac walked over and looked over Emmett's shoulder. It was a sheet of writing paper. Emmett held it long ways left to right. Across the right side was a curvy line. On the left edge someone had written the letter Z, and in several places all over the paper someone had made X's.

"What does the Z mean?" Billy Mac asked.

"What's that wavy line for?" countered Emmett, and he rotated the paper so the wavy line was now on the left side.

"What's the Z mean?" Billy Mac repeated. It was now on the right edge of the paper.

Maddie walked over to look too. "It's not a Z either way," she said after a moment. "Look. It's an N. It means north." She took the paper from Emmett and rotated it long ways up and down. The curvy line was at the bottom with an N at the top.

"You mean like a map?" Billy Mac asked.

"Sure," Maddie replied. "Look. This curvy line is the creek. We're right about here," and she pointed below the middle of the wavy line. "Boomer and I were on the other side of the creek on the edge of our field when we heard the crash."

"These X's mean something," Emmett said. "Like someone buried some stuff and made a map."

Billy Mac looked up at each of them. Finally, he asked Maddie, "What's a fancy, ritual Indian ceremony pipe doin' with a treasure map in a secret room in your great grandpa's cabin that no one's lived in for fifty years?"

Maddie looked back at Billy Mac in silence. She turned to Emmett and then back to Billy Mac. "I don't know," she finally said and smiled. "Wanna find out? You boys hungry?"

Chapter 7

Billy Mac watched Maddie's mother bustle around the farm house kitchen. She set a plate of cold fried chicken in the middle of the table next to a bowl of biscuits. Then she poured a glass of lemonade for each of the teenagers.

"Thanks, Mrs. Miller!" Billy Mac said as he reached for a chicken leg.

"You boys are lucky you weren't hurt, or worse," Mrs. Miller scolded. She dried her hands on her apron and turned on Emmett. "If your mother knew what you were doing . . ."

"Yes, ma'am," he said. "But we were very careful, Mrs. Miller. Just having some outdoor fun." He smiled at Maddie.

"Makes you glad you don't have any boys, doesn't it, Mama?" She smiled back at him.

Billy Mac watched Emmett and Maddie. *Good grief.* "So, Miss Maddie," he teased, "what were *you* doin' all the way down there by the tracks—where only boys go?"

Maddie glanced at Billy Mac, made a face, and then smiled.

Mrs. Miller stopped drying her hands, turned, and looked at Maddie. "Yes. What were you doing? You could've been hurt too!"

"Oh, Ma," she said. "Boomer and I were just hunting for arrow heads down by the creek. They're easier to find after the fields have been turned. Look, I found two this morning." She dug into her shoulder bag and then held her hand out.

Emmett reached over and took one. "Hey. This one's a spear head not an arrow head," he said. He turned it to look point-on. "See? No fluting when they made it." He drew with his fingers along each smooth side. "It can't spin like an arrow head. It's probably about nine thousand years old." He handed it back to Maddie.

Maddie tilted her head. Her hair fell from her eyes. "I know," she said. "You read it in a book, right?"

Billy Mac looked at Mrs. Miller, jerked his head toward Emmett, rolled his eyes, and shook his head.

Mrs. Miller walked over to the counter and picked up the tomahawk pipe. "This sure is something," she said. She put it back on the counter. "Did ya'll find anything else in that old cabin?"

"Oh!" Emmett cried. He jumped up and dug into a pocket. "I found this." He handed Mrs. Miller the silver frame. "I guess it would be Maddie's grandma, wouldn't it, ma'am?"

"Well, I'll be!" Maddie's mother exclaimed. "Land sakes, it must be. I don't think I have ever seen this picture. What in the world . . ."

"She sure was a pretty lady, ma'am," said Billy Mac.

"Sure was," Emmett said. "She looks just like . . ." He caught himself and blushed.

"Who's so pretty?" a voice said. Billy Mac turned to see Doc Miller walk into the room.

Maddie got up and walked to him. "Grandma was so pretty, Gramps," she answered and kissed him on the cheek. "Look what the boys found in your old cabin down by the tracks." She handed him the small, framed picture.

Doc Miller's jaw clenched. He shook his head slowly back and forth and blinked a few times.

"Do you still miss her after all these years, Gramps?" Maddie asked softly.

"Miss her every day, dear," he answered. He gave Maddie a hug, pulling her into his side. "Every single day."

Doc walked to the table, sat down, and leaned his cane against his leg. "Thank you, boys, for bringing it to us. Never did know what happened to it. Only picture I ever had of Madeline. Where'd you find it? Thought everything had been cleared out of that cabin, 'cept for the critters." He chuckled.

Billy Mac told Doc about their rail walking and finding the cabin then let Emmett finish the story with the crumbling chimney and the little room he discovered behind the hearth.

Doc Miller nodded. "There was a time or two we used that little hideaway back in the early days," he said. "A few times when an Indian was on the prowl. Never amounted to much trouble. But we kept candles back there, and whatever we didn't want stolen." He looked at the picture again and smiled. "Must have been why I took Madeline's picture back there to start with." A few moments later he looked up and said, "Find anything else?"

"Oh, yes, sir!" Billy Mac exclaimed. He got up and fetched the tomahawk pipe from the counter and held it out to Doc Miller. "Can you tell us anything about this?"

Doc Miller reached out and took the tomahawk pipe and held it still, gazing at it for several moments. Finally, he said, "This was given to my father, who was a doctor before me. It was given to him by an old Shawnee chief as a thank you for caring for him during a sick spell. I haven't thought about this for a long time." Then he repeated softly, "A long, long time, I declare."

"There's something else, sir," Billy Mac said. "Emmett, show him the map."

"Oh, right!" Emmett dug into another pocket. "That pipe was sitting on top of this." He stood up, unfolded the map, walked around the table, and handed the paper to Doc Miller, who spread it out on the kitchen table.

"We think it's a map of your farm," Emmett continued. He pointed at the curvy line at the bottom. "We think this is that big creek down by the tracks, and these"—he pointed at the X's—"are places where someone's buried some things. We think it's a treasure map of sorts."

Doc Miller nodded slowly. "Of sorts," he agreed. "Of sorts."

"You've seen this before, Gramps?" Maddie asked. She walked over and looked over his shoulder. "Do you know who drew it?"

"Hmmm? What? Do I know who drew it?" Doc asked, looking up. He smiled. "Of course I do. I did!" he said with a chuckle.

Chapter 8

Billy Mac was so startled, he couldn't speak.

"What?" Maddie asked. "You buried a bunch of stuff on the farm?"

"No," Doc Miller said. "Not buried. I was digging up. Here, let's all sit down and I'll tell you about it. Honey, go grab another chair."

Maddie came back into the room with a chair so they could all sit around the kitchen table. Billy Mac looked at the old man, waiting for him to speak.

"As I've said, my father was the first Dr. Miller, and for many years the only doctor in these parts," the old man explained, looking at those around the table. Then he leaned back and gazed past everyone. "He married as a very young man, and he and his new bride bought this land in 1840. By that time most of the Shawnee had already been moved west. A few years later, the Miami, Wea, and other tribes were moved as well. But there were some from the tribes that refused to go, a scattering here and there.

"My father built that cabin long before the railroad came through. He farmed and planted the orchard, nursed the people within riding distance when they were sick, delivered babies in the middle of the night, and sat for days on end comforting the old and the dying. He was a good man, a good husband, a good father, and a good doctor. He taught me much of what I know.

"As he told it to me, one winter night—before I was born—in the middle of a blizzard someone came knocking at that cabin door. Taking his rifle off the pegs, he opened the door to find an old Indian wrapped in blankets and sick with fever. He nursed that Indian for three days before the fever broke. Before he left, the Indian told my father—as best my father could understand in his broken understanding of their language—that as a young brave living in Prophetstown with Tecumseh, he and a band of others were taking two hundred bars of gold north to Fort Detroit and Canada to buy guns from the British. But they got into a skirmish with some American militia and had to quickly bury the gold so the Americans wouldn't find it and take it. He told my father they buried that gold somewhere on what has become the property of this farm. That would have been in, let's see, 1811 or so."

There was silence for a moment. "You mean you dug up a bunch of Injun gold on the farm?" Emmett asked.

"No," Doc answered. "I tried to. When my father first told me the story of the old Indian, I was probably about your age. There's nothing more exciting to a young man than a tale of hidden treasure, is there?" he asked with a smile.

Billy Mac looked at Emmett, who sat there wide-eyed. He could see Emmett was having a hard time containing himself. Billy Mac turned back to Doc.

"Did you ever find anything, sir?" he asked.

"No," the old man scoffed. "But not from lack of trying. I hunted for a treasure year after year. These X's"—he pointed at the map—"show everywhere I dug. I tried everywhere I thought would be a good landmark to those Indians; some of them map out places on the farm that had odd-shaped trees, some are the tops of little rises, some are by a limestone cropping popping up out of the ground. Anywhere I thought would be a good landmark—but I never found a thing."

"But your Pa," Emmett said, "he never pressed the old Indian for more information?"

"No," scoffed Doc Miller. "He never believed any of it for a minute. Said the Indians were so poor and starving at times that they would have surely dug up that gold to feed themselves. He would laugh and call my digging a fool's errand."

No one spoke for a few moments. *Two hundred bars of gold,* thought Billy Mac.

"Doc," he asked, "what would a bar of gold look like? How big would it be?"

"Well," Doc answered, "not sure, to be honest with you."

"About eight inches long, about three inches wide, about two inches high," Emmett interjected. Everyone looked at him. He gave a lopsided smile and shrugged.

"And what else?" Billy Mac asked him.

"Well, it would be very smooth to the touch," Emmett said. "Not like a normal brick that has been made out of clay. And it would be very heavy, about twenty-five pounds."

Billy Mac just shook his head at him and then turned back to Doc Miller. He picked up the tomahawk pipe.

"But what does this have to do with it all, sir?" he asked. "We found it lying on top of that drawing."

"Nothing that I know of," Doc Miller said, taking the pipe from Billy Mac. "That old Indian came back by the cabin one night a few weeks later and gave it to my father. He thought it was the old man's way of saying thank you or a form of payment. Sure is a handsome thing, isn't it?"

Everyone was silent for a minute. Finally, Maddie asked, "But, Gramps, why didn't you ever tell us about this before?"

"Because, my dear"—he smiled—"time is a great neutralizer. I had searched for Indian gold as a youngster. I never found any trace of any artifacts, certainly no gold, and then I grew into a man and life got busy. To be honest, it just faded from my mind. I don't think I ever even told your father."

"Uh, oh!" Emmett started and jumped up. "I promised Ma I'd be back by lunchtime to help do some sweeping and chores down at the Strand. I'm in for it if I don't get moving!"

Billy Mac stood up to go. "Thank you for lunch, ma'am," he said to Maddie's mother. "And thank you, Doc, for telling us about the map and pipe."

Doc Miller took his cane, stood up, and handed the map and tomahawk pipe to Billy Mac. "You boys found these. You keep them. It's my thanks for bringing us Madeline's picture."

"Gosh. Thanks, Doc!" Emmett exclaimed. "But you don't want to keep them, Maddie?"

"No," she said. "We have grandma's photo, thanks to you." She smiled at Emmett, walked over to Billy Mac, took the map from him, and handed it to Emmett. "Billy Mac should keep the pipe because he found it, and you keep this because you found it."

"Got it," Emmett answered with a nod. He turned to Mrs. Miller. "Thank you for lunch. See ya, Maddie. C'mon, Mackie."

"Boomer and I will walk as far as the creek with you," Maddie said. She reached down and rubbed between his ears. "C'mon, boy."

They walked quickly across the yard and into the plowed field toward the creek and the railroad tracks. Billy Mac was careful to walk between the newly planted rows. The turned earth smelled good. *Wonder if we're walking over the treasure right now . . . could be buried right here.*

"Was that a story or what?" Emmett broke the silence.

"Yeah! Indian gold buried right on your farm, Maddie!" Billy Mac said. "Jeez!"

"Didn't you hear him?" Maddie said. "He didn't find anything. There's nothing here; his father was right. You know that, Emmett, from all your reading. After the Indian confederacy collapsed, they were all starving. They wouldn't have left a treasure buried—if there ever was one to start with. They would have dug it up and traded for food and blankets."

"But if they had dug it up, that old Indian would have known about it," Emmett argued. "And he told Doc's pa it was still here."

"Yeah, Maddie," Billy Mac agreed. "Just 'cause Doc didn't find anything don't mean it's not still here."

"Wait a minute," Maddie said and stopped walking. Billy Mac stopped too and looked at her. She tilted her head to one side and brushed the hair out of her eyes. "Are you two telling me you want to start digging up the farm and look for buried treasure?"

She stood, hands on hips, and waited for an answer. Finally, Billy Mac said, "It won't hurt to look around."

"C'mon, Maddie." Emmett pressed her. "We need you. First, it's your family's property. Second, you know the farm inside and out. You and Boomer have romped over all these fields a thousand times. If anyone can think of a good place to bury something, it's you."

Maddie folded her arms and started walking. Billy Mac looked at Emmett, nodded after Maddie, and started walking.

When they got to the creek, Maddie climbed to the top of a large limestone cropping that jutted out of the ground at the edge of the creek bank and sat down in the shade.

"I've always loved to come here and sit with Boomer," Maddie said. She stretched her arms behind her and leaned back. "Ever since I was a little girl."

Billy Mac looked up and down the creek. Sycamore and cottonwood trees lined the banks in both directions. A faint breeze rustled the leaves. A fallen tree stretched from bank to bank as a makeshift bridge. Emmett was walking across it to the other side.

"It is a nice spot," agreed Billy Mac. He waited until Emmett reached the other side, and then he took his turn, arms sticking out as he balanced himself until he stepped off beside Emmett.

"Will you help us, Maddie?" Emmett called across the creek to Maddie.

She and Boomer still sat high on the limestone cropping on the other side. Maddie threw a few stones into the large creek.

She looked up, tilted her head, and smiled. "Sure, Emmett. I'll help you."

Billy Mac looked at the two of them and shook his head. *Good grief!*

Emmett waved to Maddie and then turned to make his way through the scrub. Billy Mac waved to her and then turned to follow Emmett.

Could we really find buried gold? Where would we start?

He made his way around the tangle of a blackberry thicket—thorns and all—then past the old cabin and up the gravel railroad bed to the tracks. Billy Mac turned for one last look at the cabin through the growth and saw someone in the shadows behind a tree. *Jeezus!*

"Look, Emmo!" he whispered. He grabbed Emmett's shoulder and spun him around.

"What? Where?" Emmett asked.

Billy Mac pointed, but there was nothing there. "I saw someone again!" he exclaimed. "I swear I did. He just disappeared."

Emmett smiled. "Mackie, you've sure got the jitters, don't you? There's no one out here. Hasn't been for fifty years. Must have been a deer or something."

"Yeah, maybe," Billy Mac said warily. He followed Emmett, walking on one of the rails with both arms out, and then paused and glanced over his shoulder. *Or maybe not.*

Chapter 9

Billy Mac lay on top of his sleeping bag and looked up at the sky. The stars were bright and plentiful. The chirping of crickets was constant.

He couldn't get his mind off of the cabin and the image of someone at the window earlier that day, or the person he was certain he saw behind the tree that had been watching them when they started on the tracks to walk home. *How could someone disappear so fast?*

He tried to picture the figure he saw in the shadows. One thing he was sure of, now that he thought about it: the person had been wearing a hat, a wide, flat-brimmed hat. *And was that a feather sticking out of the hat band? An Indian, maybe?*

It had been an old Indian that Maddie's great grandpa had doctored back to health all those years ago, the one who told the old doctor the story of buried gold. And that old Indian had come back a few weeks later to leave the tomahawk pipe. *But that was eighty years ago. That Indian can't still be alive watching over the buried gold.*

Billy Mac rolled over and looked across the porch at the black lump lying on the other sleeping bag.

"Emmo?" Billy Mac whispered.

No answer.

"Emmo!"

"Hmmm."

"You awake?" Billy Mac asked.

"Am now," Emmett mumbled. "'Sup?"

Billy Mac hesitated. "Do you believe in ghosts?"

"Don't know. Go to sleep," Emmett murmured.

"C'mon, Emmo. Do you or don't you?" Billy Mac pressed.

After a minute Emmett rolled over and sat up. "What kind of ghosts are we talking about?" he teased. "The kind that haunts houses, or the spooks that walk the earth forever in limbo 'cause they can't find their way to heaven or hell, or one of the bed-sheet haunts in a kid story? You have to be specific, Mackie."

"C'mon, Emmo!" Billy Mac shot back.

"Remember that poem we learned to recite in fifth grade for James Whitcomb Riley Day?"

"Cut it out," Billy Mac huffed. "I just wanna know if you think a person's spirit can stay around after they die—for any kind of reason. You don't have to—"

"'And just as she kicked her heels, and turned to run and hide,'" Emmett recited, "'there was two great big Black Things a-standin' by her side, and they snatched her through the ceiling before she knowed what she's about! An' the Goblins'll get you . . . if you don't . . . watch . . . out!'"

"C'mon, Emmo."

"I always did like that poem," Emmett mused.

"Okay, forget it," Billy Mac shot back. He rolled over. "Hope you roll off the porch in your sleep and break your stupid leg."

"Okay, okay," Emmett said. "Sorry, Mackie. Look, I don't know. I know a lot of people swear they've seen things or heard things that make them wonder. There's bound to be something going on that we don't understand."

Billy Mac rolled back over. "From all that readin' you do, you think there's a chance of it?"

"Yeah." Emmett shrugged. "I reckon there's a chance of it. There's supposed to be that haunted big black rock on the Wabash down past Lafayette, right?"

"And the ghost of that lady ridin' a horse down at Ghost Hollow Creek," Billy Mac added. "I ain't never seen her, but lots of people have. Pa has people come down to the jailhouse every now'n then sayin' they seen somethin'. And he says the sheriff over in Tippecanoe County gets reports of people seein' ghosts of Indians around the battleground."

"Right," Emmett replied. "And remember last year when the Hagenbeck circus train rolled in and we went down to see them unload all the animals and that big pipe organ wagon?"

"Yeah," Billy Mac said.

"We followed the parade out to the fields to watch them set up, right?" Emmett continued. "Remember the old clown we got talking to that was sitting outside his tent putting on his makeup? We asked why his clown face was a sad face. Remember what he said?"

"Yeah," Billy Mac replied. He lay down on his back and looked up at the stars. "It was because of that train wreck back in '18. All those circus folks and all those animals were burned alive. He said his sad clown face was to honor them. Said people still see ghosts around the tracks outside of Hammond."

"Yeah," Emmett answered. "Makes you think, don't it?"

The chirping of the crickets died down.

"It makes *me* think," Billy Mac said, "that *maybe* there's a ghost of that old Indian that Doc's pa treated all those years ago wanderin' around the Miller farm. Maybe still around to guard over that buried gold. And don't laugh."

"What?" Emmett asked, incredulous. "You really think you saw someone at that cabin window after that ceiling crashed?"

"Yeah, I do," Billy Mac said matter-of-factly.

"And you really think you saw someone behind that tree at the cabin when we started walking back to town," asked Emmett, "even though there was nothing there when we both looked back?"

"Yeah, I did," Billy Mac countered.

"And he looked like an old Indian to you?

"Yeah, he did," Billy Mac argued. "So what'll we do about it?"

"Well," Emmett said. "I guess we start with the only person we know that can tell us more about the Indians that lived around here. We'll go talk to Joseph. Tomorrow's Sunday and I've got work for a few days after that. We'll get down to his shop next week sometime and talk with him."

"That's more like it." Billy Mac sighed.

"Can I please go to sleep now?" Emmett asked.

"Yeah, Emmo," Billy Mac murmured. "You can go to sleep now." *I only wish I could.*

Chapter 10

"I want you to come and get it at my home tomorrow at 9:00 a.m.," the woman's voice demanded.

"Yes, ma'am," a young man's voice responded. Billy Mac sat with Emmett outside Monticello's only blacksmith shop on a bench under a sycamore tree. They couldn't avoid hearing the exchange through the open window behind them.

"And, I want the job done right."

"Yes, ma'am. I can assure you of that."

"These are very sophisticated machines. One must be qualified to properly service them."

"I agree, ma'am."

"Perhaps I should seek references."

"I am happy to provide them, ma'am. However, I assure you the work shall be done to satisfaction and your vehicle returned with punctuality."

"See that it is, young man. Your ancestry precedes you."

The woman walked out of the front door, head raised in haughty fashion, not even acknowledging the boys on the bench. Her hands gathered her skirt so as to not sweep the ground. *Good, Lord! Who in the world?* Billy Mac looked back to the doorway as their friend walked out.

At sixteen, Joseph Noble had assumed most of the day-to-day heavy work in the blacksmith shop. And why not? Billy Mac remembered the previous summer when Joseph had completed what he called his *pa-wah-kah* and had been formally accepted by the People—as Joseph referred to his tribe—into adulthood.

As with many of the People, Joseph had a tall, slim, handsome design. His trade had created a sinewy upper body. A shock of black hair descended to his dark eyes and contrasted with his snow white teeth that glowed through an ever-present smile. An easy manner made him a favorite with boys and girls alike, and his attention to detail and timely delivery made him a favorite with the elders in town. He ran a nice, neat shop.

"Hey, guys," Joseph said. He untied his leather apron and sat down on a bench across from them.

Billy Mac looked at Emmett and then back to Joseph, curious, waiting for the woman to get out of earshot.

"That, gentleman," Joseph finally said, "is the new Mrs. Skinner. Our new headmaster's bride and the new administrator for the schoolhouse when it opens in the fall."

"Jeez!" Billy Mac exclaimed. He looked at Emmett who was shaking his head, his brows furrowed.

"You amaze me, Joseph, taking that from her," Emmett said. "I don't know how you do it. I couldn't."

"Just ain't right," Billy Mac added.

Joseph smiled as usual. "I find it amusing. People like that speak out of ignorance and self-importance. I kind of feel sorry for them."

No one spoke for a minute. Billy Mac liked the morning sounds of the town. An ice wagon lumbered by, making its morning rounds.

"Joseph," Emmett started, "are you busy?"

"Just getting some things done before father gets back," he answered and waved toward the back of the shop. "Still need to finish cleaning out that room on the other side. Pa says we need the extra space to work on the autos. Getting more and more of them in all the time. What are ya'll up to?"

"Putzin' around," Billy Mac answered and looked around. "Where is your pa?"

"He went yesterday morning with a few others to track a wolf," Joseph said and shook his head. "I can't believe there's still one around here, but the tracks are plain. Been messing with some livestock, and—hey! Here comes Father now," he said, rising to his feet.

Thomas Noble drove up in a wagon. He smiled and waved at the boys, pulled up on the reins, and stopped the wagon. He set the brake and hopped down, walked over, smiled at Emmett and Billy Mac, and then turned and put his hand on Joseph's shoulder.

"*Be-zone*, Joseph. How fares the day?" he asked.

"*Be-zone, akotha*," Joseph returned the greeting. "Very, well. "I am happy to see you return." He walked over to pat the neck of the horse, Henry, and then cast a glance into the back of the wagon. The gray wolf stretched the length of the wooden bed and hung out a little over opened end. "He looks to be a great brute."

"He was that," Thomas said. "I believe the last of his kind in these parts. I will take the carcass out to Askuwheteau. He will like the hide. *Tanakia*. I shall return by sundown." He nodded to the boys, walked back to the wagon, climbed onto the bench, released the brake, and snapped the reins.

Joseph walked back to the bench. "What are you two up to today?" he asked.

Billy Mac told of their rail walking, how they found the cabin, the fallen chimney, and the hidden room behind the hearth. Emmett finished with Doc Miller's story about how his father had treated the old Indian brave, the tale of the buried gold, the map of the farm, and the tomahawk pipe.

Joseph listened, and after Emmett finished, he nodded his head. "It's a tale I'd heard growing up. The elders that were still around would sometimes speak of it, but it was nothing more than a tale. No one seemed to really believe it as far as I could tell."

"There's more," Emmett added. "Go ahead, Mackie."

"Joseph . . ." Billy Mac was unsure of how to start. He squirmed a little. "Joseph, do your people believe in spirits?"

"Oh, sure," Joseph answered. "We believe that Manitou, the most powerful of all spirits, is our connection between the People and all of nature."

"But do you believe in normal spirits, of people that have died?" Billy Mac asked with a wince.

Joseph looked at Billy Mac and then over to Emmett.

"He wants to know if you believe in ghosts," Emmett said.

Joseph looked back at Billy Mac.

Finally, Billy Mac said, "I think I saw an Indian man by the cabin when we were messin' with that chimney and then a bit later when we started back to town. But when we turned to look at him again, he'd disappeared—just vanished."

"Well," Joseph said, "to answer your question, we believe that the spirits of the dead can visit us, to guide us or to hurt us. There can be either good or evil, just like living folks."

"He thinks he might have seen the ghost of the old Indian that gave Doc's pa that tomahawk pipe all those years ago," Emmett said. "That he's out there on the Miller farm guarding over the buried Indian gold. Whooo!" He wiggled his fingers up in the air.

Billy Mac shot Emmett an angry look.

"Sorry, Mackie," Emmett said, "still trying to get my arms around this whole ghost thing."

Billy Mac scowled at him and then turned back to Joseph. "What do you think, Joseph?"

"Sure," Joseph shrugged, "I believe it is possible. I think we should seek father's counsel when he returns tonight or tomorrow, and—uh, oh, wonder what we've got going on here."

Billy Mac followed Joseph's look. A handful of young boys, all in overalls and some in bare feet, walked up the path toward them from the street. The boy in front, about ten years old, was the obvious leader. His rusty, uncombed hair framed a freckled, smudged face.

Joseph nodded at them. "Gus. Boys. How're ya'll doing?"

"Okay," the boy the in front answered. He kicked at the ground and then finally got up his nerve. "Joseph, we're wonderin' if you can help us."

"Will if I can. What's up?" Joseph said.

"Well, we're thinkin' we should try to do somethin' to get on the good side of Mrs. Skinner. You know, before schools starts so we get in good with her."

"Sounds like a good idea. What've you got in mind?"

"That's just it," one of the other boys spoke out. "We don't know what to do."

Gus said, "We saw her up here a bit ago. Thought since you talked to her you'd know what she's like and maybe can give us a good idea."

"Well . . . ," Emmett interjected.

Billy Mac looked at Emmett. *Oh, no, here he goes.*

"Emmo—," Billy Mac started.

Emmett held his hand up to cut him off. "Well, boys," he said, "I worked in that house of theirs for a few days with Mr. Skinner before he fetched Mrs. Skinner from Lafayette. I learned quite a bit from him about Mrs. Skinner."

"Emmo," Billy Mac tried again.

Emmett ignored him. "You know what Mr. Skinner told me? Her favorite color is green; she's kinda nutty about it. Wears green dresses, buys green hats. Have you boys been checking out their house?"

"Yeah," Gus said. "Been watchin' from 'cross the street, tryin' to figure out what to do for her."

"Well, you've seen, then, how Mr. Skinner had the house painted green for her?"

"Yeah," Gus answered. "Looks like they're 'bout done. Them painters jest quit for lunch."

"Well, there you go," Emmett said. "She was here just a little while ago talking to Joseph about working on her auto tomorrow—her black auto. Heard her say to him how she just loves the job the painters did and wouldn't it be grand if her car were a lovely green color to match her house."

"Hey!" Gus exclaimed. "Maybe while them painters are eatin' lunch we sneak some of that extra—"

"Nope." Emmett stopped him. "Don't tell us. Whatever you do, let it be your idea. That way she'll appreciate it all that much more."

"Gosh," Gus said, "thanks, Emmett! C'mon, guys." The boys trouped away in the direction of the Skinners' house.

Jeez! Billy Mac watched as they turned a corner and disappeared.

"You know what's gonna happen, don't you?" he asked.

"I know what should happen," Emmett said. "You heard that comment she made to Joseph about his ancestry preceding him. Whatever those boys do, she deserves it. To quote someone else, 'Justice is truth in action.' So be it."

"Those boys won't be able to sit down for a week after their pa's get done with 'em," Billy Mac said. "And they got a long, hard school year comin' up under the Skinners."

"Thanks, Emmett," Joseph said. "You know, father says the Ford Motor Company is going to come out with different colored autos for the first time later this year. But I'll bet Mrs. Skinner's will be the first green one on the street."

A green car. Jeez!

Chapter 11

Billy Mac lay on his back on top of the limestone boulder by the creek, his arms folded under his head. *Nice up here. See why Maddie likes it so much.* A warm breeze blew through the cottonwoods and flicked their disc-shaped leaves from side to side. The sound they made was like water flowing through rapids.

"So his father didn't really tell you anything new?" Maddie asked.

"Said he didn't know nothin," Billy Mac murmured. He closed his eyes. "Said the same thing that Joseph said; they'd heard stories for years but no one really gave 'em any mind."

"Hey, Mackie," Emmett called, "throw me the canteen, will you?"

Billy Mac opened his eyes, sat up, opened his backpack, took out the canteen, and threw it to Emmett. Then he took out his sketchpad and a few pencils. He opened the pad to a new page, looked up and down the creek a few times, picked up a pencil, and started sketching.

"But," Emmett added, through gulps of water, "Joseph's pa did suggest that Joseph take us to visit with an old Indian named Askuwheteau. He said if anyone knew anything about Indian gold or ghosts walking around, it would be him." He corked the canteen, set it down on the boulder, picked up a small rock, and threw it into the creek.

"And?" Maddie asked.

"And what?" Billy Mac answered. He stopped sketching and turned to the other two.

"Are you going to go talk with him?" Maddie asked.

"Yeah," Billy Mac said. He watched Emmett stand up, walk down off of the boulder, pick up a larger rock, and throw it into the creek. "He lives out in the country up on a bluff. Not too far from here, actually. Joseph's gonna take us when he has some free time. I guess they're pretty busy right now."

"I've heard Gramps talk of him before," Maddie said. A moment later she added, "I want to go with you when you do visit him. All right?"

"Yeah, sure, Maddie," Emmett answered. He was walking along the creek bank looking for something.

"Probably be a while, though," Billy Mac said. "Joseph said it would have to be after the fourth, and that's a week away."

"Will you be in town for the parade and picnic and stuff, Maddie?" Emmett called from the creek bank without turning around. "You could hang out with me and Mackie."

"Sure," she said. "My favorite part's the skyrockets. Mama and I wouldn't miss them. Gramps has to be in town too in case anyone gets burned or hurt."

Billy Mac cocked his head and watched Emmett. *What are you looking for?* Emmett stopped, picked up a very large rock with both hands, balanced it as he lifted it over his head, and threw it with a grunt into the creek. It sent a tail of water a dozen feet into the air.

"Emmett!" Maddie scolded. "What on God's green earth are you doing?"

Emmett looked up at them and smiled. "Trying to see how deep this creek is. Sounds pretty deep by the sound of the splash. What do you think, a dozen feet deep?"

"At least that right here. Gramps said there's a deep fishing hole right below us because of that stream that jets into it from the other side." Maddie pointed toward the far bank. "Says the current from that eats at this side, carving out a really deep spot."

"Deep enough to jump in then!" Emmett started pulling off his shirt.

"I wouldn't, Emmett," Maddie warned. "You won't find any place up or down for a while to get back out. The bank is pretty high up."

"Oh." He stopped and put his shirt back on.

"Anyway," Maddie said, "Gramps told me that he remembered in '08 when there was a drought. Pretty bad one, I guess. Said the creek got so low he could walk up and down the creek bed and scoop up fish that had gotten trapped in pockets of water in the deep spots. But he says it's twelve feet deep or more most of the time."

"Sure is hot," Emmett said. "A swim sure would be good." He looked up at the sky. "Could use some rain too."

"Don't think we're going to get any for a while," Maddie answered. "The almanac is calling for a long, dry summer."

"All right, you two," Billy Mac said. "Break time's over. How many more of them X's we got left to scope out?" He put his pad and pencils down and rubbed his hands over his face. "You got the map, Maddie?"

Maddie reached into her shoulder bag and pulled out the piece of paper. "Three more. Over on the far end of the field." She waved her hand toward the west.

"Don't know why we're even looking at these spots," Emmett argued. "We know your grandpa dug in those spots and didn't find anything. It's a waste of time."

"We've already talked about it," Maddie sighed. "We agreed it would help us to know the places already covered, and at the same time, it give us a good opportunity for a cross-sectional walking of the farm. It gives us a good chance to see if any other places catch our attention."

"We didn't all agree," Emmett murmured.

Billy Mac watched them argue. Maddie tilted her head and glared at Emmett. He looked back at her, over at Billy Mac, and then back to Maddie. He finally held his hands up in defense and smiled. "Okay, okay. Let's go."

Billy Mac stowed his pad and pencils, reached over and grabbed the canteen, stood up, and then he and Maddie walked down off the boulder. He looked up and down the creek and then called, "Boomer! C'mon, boy!"

Maddie's golden retriever came loping out of the shade by the creek. Billy Mac opened the canteen, cupped a hand, and poured water in it. Boomer lapped it up. Billy Mac rubbed him on the head, closed the canteen, and slung it across his shoulder.

"After you, Madam Map-keeper," Billy Mac said to Maddie.

They walked away from the creek and started across the field, careful not to step on the young cornstalks. *Knee high by the Fourth of July.* A minute later, Boomer stopped abruptly and turned toward the creek at the far end of the field.

"What is it, boy?" Maddie walked over and rubbed his ears.

They all stood looking at the line of trees. "It's nothing," Emmett called. He turned and started walking again.

"Probably a rabbit or deer," Maddie said and followed Emmett. "C'mon boy!"

Billy Mac stood by Boomer, who was still staring at the tree line. Finally, he reached down, rubbed his ears, and said, "C'mon, Boomer! C'mon!" He pulled Boomer's collar to get him walking, and they both trotted to catch up to Emmett and Maddie.

A few minutes later, a dark figure moved in the shadows from tree to tree, working its way along the opposite creek bank.

Chapter 12

The following Friday dawned a clear, hot, breezeless day. By early afternoon, wagons and a few autos filed into town to the endless crack of firecrackers (one hundred for a nickel). The sidewalks around the town square were just as crowded. Red, white, and blue banners draped most store fronts, and small children ran waving flags and stars-and-stripes pinwheels. Billy Mac sat next to Emmett in a shady spot of the courthouse lawn, watching the constant flow.

"Reckon the whole county came to town," Billy Mac said.

"Usually do," Emmett replied. "Hey, Mackie, look." He pointed down the street to an Uncle Sam in a long white beard and top hat walking on stilts. A crowd of boys threw firecrackers around the bottom of the poles until they were shooed off by a deputy.

Billy Mac saw Maddie in the distance. He nudged Emmett in the ribs and pointed.

"Hey, Maddie!" Emmett called. He stood up and waved.

Billy Mac saw her wave back. She turned, kissed her mother on the cheek, and trotted over to the boys.

"Hey, guys." She smiled as she walked up.

"Want me to take that?" Billy Mac asked. He reached up and took the picnic basket from her arm.

"Thanks," she said and plopped down in the shade next to them. "Always amazes at all the people that come in every year."

They sat for a few more minutes, pointing out people they hadn't seen since the summer before.

"Well," Billy Mac finally said, "what'dya think?"

"Yeah, we better get going," Emmett said, and he stood up.

"Where are we going?" Maddie asked, pushing herself up off of the ground.

"Over to Joseph's shop," Billy Mac answered. "He's saving the benches under the tree out front for us. We can sit there and watch the parade."

"Isn't he riding in the parade like he usually does?" Maddie asked.

"Yeah," Emmett answered, "but he's saving the benches for us—if we get there before he leaves."

When they reached the blacksmith shop, Joseph was hitching Henry to the wagon. He had fashioned an old straw hat onto the horse's head and stuck a small flag into the headband. Joseph and his father were dressed in their native finery. His brothers, sisters, and mother sat in the back of the wagon, splendid in their beaded designs. The trio walked up and exchanged hellos with the family.

"About ready to go?" Maddie asked. She walked around to rub Henry's nose.

"Just about," Joseph said. He climbed up onto the bench of the wagon and unwrapped the reins from the brake. "By the way, Father says next Saturday will be a good day for us to visit Askuwheteau. I can drive us out in the wagon. Will that work?"

"Good by me," Billy Mac said. He turned and looked at Emmett. "Emmo?"

"Yup," he replied. "We'll plan on it. Thanks, Joseph."

"I'm going too," Maddie said. "If that's okay."

"Sure," he replied. "Well, see you all at the picnic later." He snapped the reins and the wagon started. The three waved as the family rode off, and then they walked to the front of the blacksmith shop and pulled the benches to the front side of the tree.

Billy Mac turned to Maddie. "Too bad Boomer couldn't come to town with you."

"Too many firecrackers," Maddie shrugged. "And people. Better for him to stay at home."

The band started up in the distance. "Here it comes," Billy Mac said.

The streets cleared, crowds lining both sides. A few minutes later the marching band came into view, splendid in their matching uniforms. The crowd cheered as the brass section broke into the newest Sousa sensation.

The local suffragettes followed in white dresses with banners draped from their shoulders. They waved to the crowd that responded with both cheers and jeers.

Next came four perfectly matched white stallions, side by side, ridden regally by the last of the local Civil War veterans, two in blue and two in gray. The empty sleeve of one uniform was neatly pinned up because of a missing limb. Younger veterans of the Spanish-American War and the Great War followed on foot to the cheer of the crowd. Billy Mac always felt a pang for Emmett when reminders of the Great War came up. Emmett's father went to the Somme in 1918 with First Division's Twenty-Eighth Infantry and never came home.

The volunteer fire department followed the soldiers and showcased their new steam engine. Cheers turned to laughter when the stilted Uncle Sam walked by with a determined throng of young boys throwing firecrackers at his stick feet.

Wagons and people on horseback brought up the rear. Billy Mac picked up Maddie's basket, and the three joined in as the crowd filtered in behind the pageant, trooping down Main Street to the park for picnics and games.

"Over there." Maddie pointed to a flat spot under a shady sycamore. She took the basket from Billy Mac, opened it, removed a red-and-white checkered tablecloth from the top, and spread it on the ground.

Billy Mac sat on one corner of the tablecloth, Emmett sat on another, Maddie on yet another, and then she set the picnic basket right in the middle.

"Watcha got in there, Maddie?" Billy Mac asked as he leaned over and peaked in the basket.

"Well, I'll show you." She reached in and took out a covered plate. She folded the cloth back to reveal deviled eggs sprinkled with paprika.

"My favorite!" Billy Mac exclaimed as he reached for one and plopped the whole thing in his mouth. *Oh, my gosh!* He reached for another.

"Good," Maddie replied as she set the plate down on the tablecloth and reached into the basket again. She took out another covered plate, unwrapped the cloth, and set it on the ground.

"*My* favorite!" Emmett leaned over and picked up a fried chicken leg.

"I know." She smiled at him. Emmett took a bite and smiled back.

Sheesh! Billy Mac watched the two of them and shook his head.

"Gosh, Maddie," Billy Mac said, "we should have brought something to share with you."

"Not needed," she replied. She reached into the basket and took out rolls, a jar of pickles, some smoked ham, and a bowl of cobbler. It was still warm. "Boomer and I picked these blackberries yesterday."

After they ate, the three walked around the park. Some kids threw a baseball, and others lay on blankets playing puzzle peg or dominos. Some of the adults played croquet.

Evening approached and the band gathered into the large gazebo at the center of the park for the celebration concert. As it got dark, young and old alike lit sparklers and drew imaginary figures and designs in the air with their white sparks and smoke trails.

Finally, from the far side of the river, the first skyrocket flew into the air; a red shower pushed it higher and higher. It exploded, and another followed—and then another and another.

The air was thick from gunpowder smoke. Billy Mac watched and his mind wandered back to that day at the cabin when the air was thick from the dust cloud of the collapsing chimney. He thought about the silhouette of the person he'd seen at the cabin window through that cloud of dirt and then again as he and Emmett began their walk back to town on the railroad tracks. *That felt hat—wide, flat brim, feather sticking up out of the hat band . . .*

Then through the smoke he saw the same image fifty yards away, that same silhouette sticking out past a tree. *It can't be!* Billy Mac blinked and made a useless attempt of waving smoke away for a better look. He jumped up and worked his way toward that tree. He never heard Emmett or Maddie calling after him.

Billy Mac stumbled through the haze and tried to keep sight of the image but had to look away again and again to keep from running into others in the crowd who were watching the fireworks. He finally reached the tree but saw no one. *No! I lost him!* Then a skyrocket exploded and the flash showed the figure melting into the thick smoke cloud toward the river bluff at the front of the park. Billy Mac wove through the crowd as fast as possible. When he reached the edge of the bluff, he saw nobody. *No! Not again!* Skyrocket after skyrocket exploded; it was the grand finale. Billy Mac squinted and peered down through the smoke to the river bank in both directions, but the resounding flashes that lit up the haze showed nothing.

Chapter 13

Billy Mac sat on the back of the wagon bed, his legs hanging off. Emmett sat next to him. Behind them, up on the wagon bench, Joseph snapped the reins and the wagon jolted to a start. "C'mon, Henry. Let's go," he said.

Billy Mac turned around to look. Maddie sat next to Joseph on the bench. Boomer lay in the front of the wagon bed, behind the bench.

"How far is it, Joseph?" Maddie asked.

"Not far. About ten minutes or so," Joseph answered. "Have to cross the river and then follow it north a ways. He lives up on the bluffs."

"Hey!" Emmett called. "Did anyone bring water? It's gonna be a hot one."

"Sure did," Joseph replied without turning around. "A couple of canteens up here under the bench." He snapped the reins again, guiding the horse across the wooden planks of the bridge, its hooves clip-clopping in time. "Okay, someone give me an update of the past few weeks."

"I'll give you an update!" Maddie snapped. "No ghosts and no gold!"

"Aw, Maddie," Billy Mac said. "Look, Joseph, we've crisscrossed the farm a few times. We found all the places that Maddie's grandfather dug when he was a boy, everywhere marked on the map. We've tried some other places on our own. But there's still a lot more places to look. It's a very large farm."

"No ghosts and no gold," Maddie repeated. She turned around and smiled. Billy Mac forced a smile and turned back around to face the road behind them.

"And no more sightings of ghosts or spirits?" Joseph asked.

"Nope!" Emmett and Maddie answered at the same time. Then Emmett added, "Well, maybe the night of the fireworks."

"C'mon, guys," Billy Mac said in defense. "I'm tired of talking about it." He lay back into the wagon bed, his arms under his head to cushion it from the bouncing as the wagon rattled along.

The horse walked off of the bridge and Joseph turned him north onto a gravel road that ran along the river bank.

"So let me get this straight," he said so Billy Mac and Emmett could hear him. "Billy Mac believes there is both buried gold and the spirit of an old Indian wandering Doc's farm."

"Right!" Emmett and Maddie answered.

"Emmett," Joseph continued, "believes there is buried gold but no ghost."

"Right," Emmett said. Billy Mac rolled his head to the side and opened one eye to glare at him. Emmett looked down at Billy Mac and shrugged. "Sorry, Mackie."

"And Maddie," Joseph said, "doesn't believe in either."

"Right!" Maddie answered. "No gold and no ghosts."

"Got it," Joseph said. "So what do you do next?"

"Not sure," Billy Mac said without getting up. He had put his hat over his face to protect it from the sun. "The ground's so hard from no rain that we can't really dig no more."

Thankfully, Maddie changed the subject. "Joseph, tell us about who we're going to see. How do you pronounce his name, again?"

"ASK-u-WHET-oh," he said. "He garners much respect and is considered a chieftain among the People. He is very wise. We're getting close to his cabin."

"Don't think I've ever seen 'em," Billy Mac said, his hat still covering his face.

"He lives as closely as possible as our customs state with Manitou," Joseph explained. "He lives with mother earth—a simple life. Father brings him the few things he needs from town and checks on him from time to time."

Billy Mac sat up. The road had forked away from the river bluff. Joseph slowed the wagon and turned onto a small side road. It was little more than a grassy lane lined on both sides by tall oaks, sycamores, and cotton woods. *Nice here in the shade.* He reached behind him and rubbed Boomer between the ears and then lay back down, his arms under his head. *Will this old Indian know anything? If he does, will he tell us? Maybe he will since Joseph's with us.*

The cicadas had finally come out with the full heat of the summer. Their staccato drone started low, picked up in pitch, and then rolled back to a lull. Eee-eee-eee-AH-AH-AH-AH-AH-AH-AH-EE-EE-eh-eh-eh-eh-eh. Billy Mac allowed the hypnotic sound to lull him away from the conversation of the others.

"Here we are," Joseph finally called. Billy Mac snapped back to awareness and sat up.

The wagon rounded a bend in the lane and they approached a small log cabin. The path dead-ended right before it. The cabin sat on the edge of a high bluff, overlooking the Tippecanoe River. A cliff rose behind it and along one side, protecting it from the north and east. Cotton woods shaded the cabin, their leaves flickering in the breeze that rolled off the river and up the bluffs.

"Be-zone, akotha," Joseph called from the wagon bench. He set the brake, wrapped the reins loosely around the brake handle, and jumped down from the wagon.

Billy Mac looked, and for the first time he noticed a small man sitting on a bench in the shade at one corner of the cabin. He was dressed in an old flannel shirt that hung loose on his small frame. His dungarees ended above his ankles and he wore no shoes. His long, gray hair was tied in the back so that it fell down his back. His ancient face was that of brown, wrinkled leather.

"*Be-zone, peshewa*," the old man replied with slow deliberation. "And *be-zone* to the *hileni* and *kweewa* that accompany thee." He nodded to others.

Joseph motioned to them. "May I present my friends Emmett, Billy Mac, and Maddie Miller. She is the granddaughter of Doctor Miller, whom you know."

Joseph then motioned toward the old man. "My friends, allow me to introduce Askuwheteau, an elder and chief among the People."

Billy Mac smiled and nodded, not quite sure what to do with the formal introductions. He and Emmett stood up from the back of the wagon bed and walked over to stand with Joseph. Maddie, however, stepped down from the wagon, walked over to the old man, and with a feint curtsy said, "*Be-zone*, Askuwheteau. It is an honor."

"And by what name do we call the *wii'si*?" Askuwheteau asked and motioned toward the wagon bed.

"Oh!" cried Maddie. "Here, boy!" She clapped her hands and the retriever bounded from the wagon. "This is Boomer, my companion for as long as I can remember."

Askuwheteau reached out a wrinkled hand to let Boomer get his scent. "Yes, we shall be good friends, won't we *wii'si*?" He patted the dog's head. "And of your father." He looked at Joseph. "How fares *Topeah*?"

"Very well, thank you," replied Joseph. He sat on the bench next to the old man. "*Akotha*," he continued, "my friends would seek your council on matters."

"My council?" the old man repeated. He nodded his consent. "Then you must all come and sit."

Emmett nudged Billy Mac and nodded toward a bench on the opposite corner of the cabin. They picked it up and carried it back to sit across from Askuwheteau. Maddie sat down next to them.

"What council would you seek from an old man?" Askuwheteau addressed them with a smile. He reached into his shirt pocket and pulled out a wooden pipe and a bag of tobacco.

"Emmett," Joseph said, "why don't you start with what you found in Doctor Miller's old cabin?"

Emmett explained how they happened across the cabin, caused the felling of the chimney, and discovered the room behind the hearth.

Billy Mac told him about the map drawing they found and the markings on it, and Maddie explained the story that her grandfather told them about the gold and how he had searched for it as a boy. She concluded in sharing her grandfather's opinion that the gold wasn't there any longer—if it ever existed at all.

Billy Mac studied the old man. *Do you know anything? Would you tell us if you did?* Through the briefing Askuwheteau had sat in contemplative silence, nodding from time to time. When Maddie finished, the silence continued for a moment.

Finally, the old man spoke. "And the other matter you would seek council on? You mentioned yet another?"

Billy Mac squirmed. He looked at his friends. He clenched his jaw, not sure how to start.

"Well, sir," he said, "I-I get the feeling that sometimes when we've been searching Doc's farm we're being watched."

He looked at Maddie. She tilted her head and squinted at him to tell the rest.

"And that maybe whoever it is could be a-a ghost that wanders around in that area." He looked at Emmett, who nodded his head once and then jerked his head toward the old Indian, prodding him to go on.

Billy Mac continued. "We . . . I wonder if it could be the spirit of the old chief that was treated by Doc's father so many years ago, that first told him the story of the buried gold. Perhaps his spirit remains to guard over it." He finished and grimaced. He looked at Joseph who gave him a nod of approval.

The cottonwood leaves rustled and the smoke from Askuwheteau's pipe circled and rose into the trees. The cicada's droned higher and then dropped off.

"I see," Askuwheteau said. Then he sat in silence and drew slowly on his pipe. "I see," he repeated. He took a stick, poked at the fixings in the pipe, and then turned it over and tapped it on the bench so that the spent ashes fell to the ground.

"And you would seek my council? You wonder if there is truth to these matters?" he asked.

"Yes, sir," Billy Mac answered.

Askuwheteau pulled the tobacco bag from his shirt pocket again and filled the pipe. When he finished, he looked up. "Yes. There is truth to the tale of the gold, yet none know all there is to know except myself." He nodded toward Billy Mac. "And you are wise to believe in the spirits of those gone before. Even when others would not." He looked at Emmett and Maddie. "For some have a purpose in their life that continues in their death."

"You, *akotha*?" Joseph asked. "How is it that you should know of such things, of the gold, of things none of the other elders know?"

"Because," the old man answered, "the chieftain of the People that passed the legend on to your great-grandfather"—he nodded toward Maddie—"so many years ago was my father."

Chapter 14

Stunned by what the old man told them, no one spoke. The smell of pipe tobacco was heavy in the air.

His father—no way! Billy Mac shook his head and at looked at the others.

Finally, Maddie said, "But, Askuwheteau, how can that be? It must be at least eighty years since my great-grandfather treated the old chieftain. That would make you . . ."

"A very old man, my young *ikwe*," Askuwheteau said. "I am a very old man. But first, to know the story of the gold, you must first know the story of the People and that of the Shooting Star—the story of Tecumseh."

Askuwheteau tamped his pipe on the bench. Ashes fell to the ground and he scrubbed them over with his bare foot. He laid the pipe on the bench, put both hands forward on his knees, and looked up into the trees.

"He was not the first to bring the tribes together. A hundred and fifty years ago the People were being pushed more and more off of their lands by the whites." Askuwheteau grunted. "The whites! Ever thirsty for more and more lands and never truthful in their words. No honor in their leaders." He shook his head.

"Before the year 1800, the mighty war chief Blue Jacket and the great Little Turtle rallied their tribes together to fight the whites in the lands of Ohio. They had victories, but in the end met with defeat. Once again, the People were forced to cede their homelands to the whites and were pushed west. And once more, the whites broke their promises.

"Then came the Shooting Star, and then came Tecumseh and his confederacy of tribes. Ah, what a man! There never was one more *wil-li-thie*—never one more handsome. And he was a leader among all men—even the whites. When he walked into council, all stood quiet in awe of him. When he spoke, all listened. And, oh, how he spoke! For hours he held council of the People with the whites in his hands, and all listened to his wisdom. How close he came to peaceful resolve. When he finally knew in his heart that the whites would break their promises yet again, he moved his tribe from Ohio into Indiana, not far from here. There, where the mighty Wabash meets its little brother"—he pointed below to the Tippecanoe River—"he founded Prophetstown, and he would be pushed no more.

"He remembered Blue Jacket and Little Turtle uniting tribes when he was but a young man. But he had something they did not have; he had his brother, Tenskwatawa—he had the Prophet. The Great Spirit had come to Tenskwatawa in a waking dream and told him to gather all the people together and return to the ways of Manitou and Mother Earth. They were to take nothing from the whites, to give up living like the whites, to eat only of what was provided by Mother Earth. For if they did so, they could defeat the white devils. So while Blue Jacket and Little Turtle only had the anger of the People to unite them, when Tecumseh brought all together again, he also had religion to fire the fever of the People.

"He traveled far, to the lands of the New York Iroquois, south to the Chickasaw, and even to the great Gulf and west to the Sioux of the Black Hills. Tecumseh took the words of the Prophet, and with his gifted speech, many joined him, returning to Prophetstown and transforming it into a large, populous center to fight the white encroachment.

"Tecumseh allied his confederacy with the British, who agreed to return tribal lands upon defeat of the Americans. It was for this reason that he gathered gold from the Sioux, to buy guns from the British. My father and other warriors took this gold and began their journey north to the British from Prophetstown. Shortly into their journey, they happened on American soldiers and were forced to abandon the gold so it would not be captured by the enemy. There it remains to this day, awaiting the time for it to be used to regain homelands for the People."

"But Tecumseh was killed in Canada in 1813," interjected Emmett. "And that was the end of the confederacy."

"Yes," Askuwheteau answered, "but it was not the end of the dream."

"But for years your people suffered, starving at times," Maddie added. "Surely, the gold would have been recovered to buy food and blankets and clothing for your people."

"No, it would not have been," Askuwheteau answered.

"But why not?"

"Because, my young *ikwe*," he explained, "Tecumseh had declared the gold to only be used to fight the whites. Each warrior in the band took an oath. It would not be used for any other purpose, not even to feed the starving."

"But that's just wrong!" Maddie cried. She crossed her arms with a huff.

"Then, sir, you believe it is still there?" Billy Mac asked.

"It is still there," Askuwheteau replied. "It still waits to be used for the People, to help them reclaim what they have lost."

"Do you know where it is, Askuwheteau?" Emmett meekly asked.

"I do not," he replied. "No one does."

"How is it that no one knows, *akotha*?" Joseph asked.

"The band of warriors that accompanied the gold north to the British was twenty in number," Askuwheteau explained. "Only they knew its resting place. One by one they each died in battle or became ill as they aged until only a few were left. The few agreed that the last of them would become the Watcher; the last one would keep safe watch over the resting place of the gold. Before his death the Watcher would find one to pass the secret to but only after the chosen one swore to the same oath that all swore to in the beginning. Thus was the plan to keep the gold safe until it could fulfill its purpose."

"But your name, *akotha*," Joseph said slowly. "Askuwheteau, it means 'the Watcher' in the language of the People."

"Yes, *peshewa*," the old man answered. "My father was the last survivor of the original band. When I was born, that was the name given to me by him. I was to be the Watcher after his *nep-poa*. I was to safeguard the resting place. It was to fall to me."

"But," Billy Mac started, "it didn't? Your father never passed it on to you?"

"He tried, *mean-e-lench*," Askuwheteau explained. "But I was young and headstrong. I wanted him to tell me of the hiding place, but I would not swear to the oath he demanded. Young men dream of wealth, and so it was with me. I was maddened that I could not have it. Like many *mi-a-nie*, I had no wisdom; so young was I. My *ot-to-hie* was dark and filled with anger. And so I left and wandered for many years. As I became older and wiser, I came to understand the truth of Tecumseh's oath and returned. But by that time, my father had died. And with him died the secret of the gold's resting place."

All sat in silence. Billy Mac stood up and walked to the edge of the bluff and looked down at the river. The warm breeze flickered through the cottonwoods and the drone of the cicada's rose in pitch. *So we'll never know. The farm is too big. It could be anywhere.* He turned and faced the others.

Once again, Maddie broke the silence. "Askuwheteau, I believe your father tried to pass the information on. He told my great-grandfather about the buried gold. Your father might have told him a detailed location, but my great-grandfather didn't understand the language of the People well enough. He only understood that it was buried someplace on the farm. Wouldn't your father have written the location down or made a map to pass the information on to others if he thought he was going to die before he could find a new Watcher?"

"I thought of that as well," the old man said. "For many years after my return I searched for where he might have left a hidden clue, for he would not have left it for just anyone to find. But I gave up hope long ago. And it is not wise to dwell on things that cannot be."

Billy Mac walked back to the bench and sat down. *There's really nothing we can do then. Is he telling us everything he knows?* He studied Askuwheteau's ancient face, searching for a clue. The old Indian reached into his shirt pocket for the strings of his tobacco bag and pulled it out. He picked up his pipe and tapped it against the wooden bench to clear it and began to fill it again.

Maddie reached over and touched Billy Mac's arm. "We should have brought that pipe that Askuwheteau's father gave to my great-grandfather. He would probably like to see it."

The change in Askuwheteau was immediate. He gasped and the color drained from his face. He dropped the pipe and tobacco bag to catch himself from falling off the bench.

Joseph jumped to his aid and steadied him. "*Akotha, akotha*, are you ill? Here, lie down!" He helped the old man lie down on the bench. He turned to Billy Mac. "Water, hurry. Around the side!" He waved toward the corner of the cabin.

Billy Mac ran around the side of the cabin and found the well in the shade of the trees. He dropped the bucket and heard the splash. He waited a few seconds and then drew the rope through the pulley until he had the bucket back in his hands. He took the ladle from the post where it hung and dipped out some cool water. He pulled his bandana out of his pocket, soaked it in the bucket, and then hurried back to the front of the cabin as fast as he could without spilling. "Here!" He handed the bandana to Joseph.

The old man lay with his eyes closed, but his breathing was steady. Joseph put the cold, wet bandana on Askuwheteau's forehead and then softly wiped both sides of his face. The old man opened his eyes. "It is well," he said softly.

Maddie took the ladle from Billy Mac and stooped next to the bench. "Here, try to take a drink." She put her hand under his head and softly lifted until he was able to sip.

Askuwheteau blinked a few times and forced a smile. "It is well," he repeated. "Help me to sit."

Joseph and Maddie helped him up. "Slowly, *akotha*," Joseph said.

The old man sat up on the bench. Emmett picked up the little wooden pipe and the tobacco bag. He brushed them off and laid them on the bench next to the old man. Even Boomer nudged forward. Askuwheteau reached down and rubbed him between the ears. "All is well, *wii'si*. Do not be alarmed."

Maddie and Joseph sat on either side of him. Billy Mac sat back down on the bench across from them, next to Emmett.

The old Indian turned toward Maddie. "You must forgive me, but the shock was great. You say that my father gave a pipe and to your grandfather's father?"

Maddie's eyes were wide. "Yes," she said softly.

"This pipe is not an ordinary smoking pipe as such?" he asked, holding up his small wooden pipe.

She tilted her head to let the hair fall from her eyes. "No," she answered.

"And, my young *ikwe*," the old man continued, "it is long and carved and painted? It looks to be a weapon, a tomahawk, but it is a pipe?"

"Yes!" Maddie gasped. "But how could you know that?"

"A simple guess." He shrugged. "And now, my young friends, I think this old man should rest. Will you visit again soon and bring the pipe my father gave the young doctor so many years ago? I should like to see it."

Billy Mac looked at his three friends. "The pipe's in my backpack at my house. I can come out any time. I can work my chores around it. Just need to keep Morris's stocked with eggs and tomatoes."

"I've got work the next three or four days," Emmett said. "But I can come after that."

Maddie shrugged. "I can come back any time, if you all will come and pick me up in the wagon. Mama won't mind."

Billy Mac looked at Joseph. "I'll check with father," he said. "He won't mind if I'm gone for a few hours some evening after supper. I'll check with him as soon as we return to town."

A large rock dislodged itself somewhere from the side of the cliff wall across from the cabin and rolled through the trees, the noise of it loud as it crunched through the underbrush. Boomer was up at once, pointing toward the corner of the cliff that turned by the grassy lane. He growled and bared his teeth.

Billy Mac was the first to jump up. He ran toward the sound. He stopped before entering the trees, straining to look into the shadows. He was certain he saw something slip quickly around the corner of the cliff. *Here we go again. Jeez!* He shook his head in frustration.

He walked back over to Boomer, reached down with both hands, and scratched the dog's ears. "It's okay, boy. It's gone—whatever it was." He glanced behind him and then took Boomer by the collar and walked back to the benches.

"More ghosts, Mackie?" Emmett asked.

Billy Mac frowned and shrugged his shoulders.

"Okay," said Joseph, "we should probably be getting Maddie home."

They each said their good-byes to the old man and loaded back onto the wagon. Maddie sat beside Joseph again on the bench. Billy Mac and Emmett sat on the back of the wagon bed, their legs hanging off. The wagon turned onto the grassy lane, and Billy Mac looked into the trees at the bottom of the cliff and then up to the ridge at the top. *What were you? Are you still watching us?*

Chapter 15

Emmett shook his head. He stood in the street and looked up the walk to the blacksmith shop. He could hear voices inside. *Wonder what she wants, now?*

He took a couple of steps to find the shelter of shade on the bench. Then the door flung open so hard it snapped against the outside wall. Mrs. Skinner shoved her way past Emmett, huffing and puffing. "No-good, lazy, shiftless," she muttered as she stomped down the walk.

Emmett turned back to see Joseph in the open doorway. Joseph shrugged his shoulders, looked up at the sky, and shook his head. He rolled his eyes and then walked back into the shop.

Emmett frowned and followed him in. "Hey, did you know you're no-good and lazy?" he asked Joseph.

"Yes. And don't forget shiftless," Joseph answered without looking up. He tied his leather apron on, picked up a slug of iron with his tongs, and put it in the bed of coals. He pumped the bellows a few times. It didn't take long for the slug to start glowing around the edges.

"I can't stand it, Joseph," Emmett said.

Joseph looked up and smiled. "It's okay, Emmett. I've put up with worse from better people. She's not worth it."

"What was it about this time?" Emmett asked.

Joseph thumbed toward the side shop through the door. "Wanted me to get all that green paint off of her auto. Thinks I ought to be able to get it all off, no problem, just like new." He shook his head. "That's impossible."

"So it's your fault, huh?" Emmett grunted. "Man, that makes me mad!"

Joseph chuckled. "Has to be someone's fault, I suppose."

"What'd she leave it here for, then? Why didn't she drive it home?" Emmett asked.

"She wants father to look at it. Believes he will see it differently than me," Joseph answered.

"No way of that," Emmett said and shook his head. "Where is he anyway? You can still take us out to Askuwheteau's, right?

"Yes. Father will be here in a few minutes. As soon as Billy Mac gets here we can leave. We'll pick up Maddie on the way. I already have Henry hooked up to the wagon." He nodded to the back door of the shop. "We can—hey. Here comes Billy Mac now."

Emmett followed Joseph's look through the front window. He watched Billy Mac walk up from the street. He was carrying a large basket full of tomatoes. Billy Mac didn't even look up as he came through the doorway; he just pushed his way past Emmett into the shop. He was visibly unhappy. He put the basket down on a workbench.

"What's up?" Emmett asked him.

Billy Mac looked at him and then to Joseph. "You ain't gonna believe this. You just ain't gonna—"

"Hey, Emmett. Hey, Joseph." A voice interrupted them.

Emmett turned toward the door and saw Gus standing in the doorway with his gang behind him.

"Hey, Gus," Joseph said. "How're you all doing? Come on in."

One by one the younger boys shuffled in. Emmett waited and then asked, "What's up, guys?"

Gus looked uncomfortable. "It's that Skinner woman. She's gonna be makin' life hell for us."

"Yeah?" Emmett asked. "How so?"

"Well, we tried to do something nice for her. Painted her car for her and did it for free; she didn't ask for nothin'. Just got us all a good tannin' instead."

"Yeah?" Emmett mocked surprise.

"Yeah," Gus said. "Then we tried to be nice to her anyways. Gone up to her house a few times asking if we could help with any chores. She was just plain mean tellin' us not to set foot on her property again and to just wait till school starts, that she'd sure show us then. It's gonna be hell, pure and straight." Gus dug his hands into his overall pockets, hung his head, and shook it back and forth. "We just don't know what to do. We sure owe her for the way she's been treatin' us."

Emmett stood there for a minute thinking, and then he smiled. "Well," he said, "you can't do anything to her unless you do it without her knowing it was you."

"Emmo," Billy Mac interrupted.

Emmett waved him off. He walked over to the work bench and picked a tomato out of Billy Mac's basket. He walked back over in front of the boys and tossed it up and down a few times. "If you're looking for a way to show her what's what, you've got to be smart. You've got to get her in a way that she can't know it was you." He tossed the tomato up and down a few more times.

"Emmo."

Emmett ignored Billy Mac.

"We'd sure like to show her," Gus grumbled and turned to look at his small gang. "Wouldn't we guys?" The boys all nodded and murmured consent. "She ain't got no reason to get so nasty with us. We was just trying to be nice to her."

Emmett tossed the tomato higher, catching it with both hands and then tossing it up high again.

"Well . . . ," he started. He caught the tomato with both hands and then reared back and threw the tomato with all his strength—like a baseball—into a metal drum barrel in the corner. The tomato hit the inside with an echoing boom and exploded. The splattered effect was dramatic. Emmett turned back to face the boys. Their eyes were wide and transfixed.

"Her automobile is out back in Joseph's shop," Emmett continued with a smile. "She has to walk everywhere she goes. Over to the schoolhouse and then back home. Down to town and then back home. You boys will think of something."

"Yeah," Gus said. His eyes narrowed a little. "We will. C'mon, guys." He walked out with the others trailing in line.

Emmett watched them go and then turned to his two friends. "Sorry, Mackie. Mrs. Skinner stomped out of here right before you showed up. She deserves every bit of it."

Emmett looked at Joseph who smiled and simply said, "Thanks."

Emmett gave Joseph a slight nod and then turned back to Billy Mac. "Okay, Mackie, what's wrong?"

Billy Mac shook his head back and forth. "You just ain't gonna believe it. The pipe's gone. My backpack that I keep all my stuff in, the whole thing's gone—stolen!" He shook his head, threw up his arms in disbelief, and sat down on the edge of the workbench.

Chapter 16

Billy Mac sat with the others around Maddie's kitchen table at the farm. He'd just finished telling her about the stolen pipe and backpack. *Still can't believe it.* He shook his head and reached down and scratched Boomer between the ears.

"Are you sure you didn't just leave it somewhere else?" Maddie asked.

Billy Mac frowned. "C'mon, Maddie," he answered. "I know where I left my backpack. I always leave it on a little table in my bedroom with my pocket knife and stuff." He patted his pants pocket.

"Did you sleep with your window open last night?" she asked.

"'Course I did; it's been so blamed hot," Billy Mac answered.

Emmett straightened up in his chair. "You mean, someone snuck through your window while you were sleepin', took the backpack, and snuck back out?"

"Looks that way," Billy Mac answered.

"Did your father do some looking around?" Joseph asked.

"Yeah, when I realized it was missin' I went down to the jailhouse and told him 'bout it," Billy Mac answered. "He came back home with me and looked around. That side of the house is always shaded and the ground next to the house is usually a little softer. He said he thought he could see some footprints."

"That's it? That's all?" Emmett asked.

"No. There's more," Billy Mac said softly and lowered his head. "He said whoever did it wasn't wearin' normal shoes. There wasn't no heal mark dug into the ground. They was wearin' flat, soft soles—like moccasins."

No one said anything. He raised his head and looked at the others.

Emmett was the first to finally speak. "Mackie, ghosts don't leave footprints."

"I know."

"And, not many people around here wear moccasins," Emmett murmured.

"Only a few that I know of," Joseph said. "And those are of the People."

"But we're missing the point," Maddie exclaimed. "The question is why would someone steal that backpack? For the pipe? Why? And who would have known about it anyway?"

Billy Mac looked at Joseph. *Only one other person knows about it.*

"It couldn't have been," Joseph said. "He's not a thief. He's an honorable old man."

Billy Mac forced a smile and nodded.

"It just doesn't add up," Emmett said.

"He knew we were going to bring it to him sometime soon," Maddie said. She tilted her head and brushed the hair out of her eyes. "So let's go see him. We'll tell him it's been stolen and see what he says."

Billy Mac nodded. He looked at the other boys. Emmett and Joseph murmured their agreement

Maddie stood up. "'C'mon, Boomer, let's go," she said and headed for the kitchen door.

Chapter 17

The wagon bounced up the grassy lane to Askuwheteau's cabin. Everyone sat in their usual spots: Maddie beside Joseph on the bench, Billy Mac and Emmett on the back of the wagon bed, facing the road behind them, and Boomer lay in the wagon bed behind the bench.

The sun beat down from a cloudless sky and Billy Mac was sweating. *God, I wish it would cool off and rain. We need it, bad.*

They rounded the corner of the cliff wall, and Billy Mac looked up into the trees where he had seen the shadow slip away during their first visit. *Are we being watched, again?* His concentration was broken by Joseph's hail.

"Be-zone, akotha," Joseph called.

Billy Mac hopped off the wagon bed and turned to walk to the cabin. Askuwheteau was standing beside the bench next to the front door. He had a leather bag into which was packing different items.

He looked startled to see them. "*Be-zone* to you, my friends," he said. "I did not expect to see thee so soon." He quickly put the rest of the items in his bag and closed the drawstring; then he sat down on a bench.

Boomer bounded out of the wagon over to the old man, who rubbed his head. Maddie, Joseph, and Emmett climbed from the wagon and walked over.

A walking stick leaned up against the bench and next to the leather bag was a wide-brimmed felt hat with a feather sticking out of the hatband. *Jeezus!* Billy Mac was transfixed, his heart beating faster.

"We came to give you news," he heard Joseph say.

Billy Mac looked up and caught Joseph's and Emmett's attention. He nodded at the hat, not sure what to do or say.

Emmett looked back at Billy Mac and then at the hat and turned to the old man. "The pipe we spoke of, it has been stolen, Askuwheteau," he said. "It was taken from Billy Mac's house last night, along with the backpack in which it was kept."'

"I see," the old man said with a sigh. He looked down at the ground. "It is most unfortunate. I am sorry for your loss."

Everyone stood in silence.

"It looks as if you are readying to leave, *akotha*," Joseph said. "We have stopped to visit at a bad time."

"'Tis nothing, *peshewa*. I am going to take a walk in the countryside," Askuwheteau replied. He looked up. "This stolen pack, do you hope to find it? Is there suspect of the thief?"

"Not at this time." Joseph shook his head.

Everyone stood in silence.

I can't stand it, Billy Mac thought. Finally he said, "Well, we need to be going. We need to get you home, right, Maddie?"

"Oh! Yes, that's right; we should be going," Maddie said. "C'mon, boy." She reached out to scratch Boomer. "Good-bye, Askuwheteau." She turned and started toward the wagon. Billy Mac, Joseph, and Emmett murmured a good-bye to the old man and followed her.

"Good-bye, my friends," the old man replied softly.

The wagon bumped down the grassy lane. Once they left the shade the sun beat down relentlessly. Billy Mac took his hat off and wiped his forehead. *What'll we do now?*

No one spoke. After a few minutes, Joseph turned the wagon onto the gravel road.

"Stop a minute, Joseph," Billy Mac heard Maddie say. He twisted around to face the bench. Emmett did the same.

Joseph reined the horse to a stop, set the brake, and wrapped the reins around brake handle. He and Maddie both turned to face Billy Mac and Emmett.

"What does everyone think about that?" she asked.

"Very strange," Emmett said. "When we were here before he was very talkative. Today he was short with us, like he couldn't get rid of us fast enough." He looked at Billy Mac.

"I agree with Emmo," Billy Mac said. "Plus, his hat that was sittin' on the bench. The person I've seen three times? He was wearin' a hat just like it. And did you see what Askuwheteau was wearin' on his feet?"

"Moccasins," answered Maddie. They all looked at Joseph.

He nodded a few times, a frown on his face. "I agree he acted strangely, but Askuwheteau is no thief. Besides, why would he have stolen the pipe? He knew we were going to bring it out to him."

"That's just it," Billy Mac argued. "He knew to expect us, right? That's what we told him. And he really wanted to see that pipe. Then how come he was leavin' without waitin' to see it? He ain't going for a short walk. And if we'd a got there a few minutes later, he'da been long gone." He turned to look at Emmett who nodded back at him.

"I think there's something about that pipe that he's not letting on to," Emmett said. "And I agree with Mackie. Did you see that bedroll on the other bench on the far side of the door? He's planning on being gone a few days and sleeping out. He couldn't wait for us to leave."

"I agree that a mystery seems to surround the pipe," Joseph said. "Although, strange as it may be, I still say he's no thief."

Everyone sat in silence. Finally Maddie spoke. "I agree with Joseph. He clearly has something that he was preoccupied with, but it doesn't make sense that he would walk into town, sneak into your house while you were sleeping, and steal your backpack."

"Okay, that's fine," Billy Mac said. "Let's just leave it at that. Let's just agree that we all keep our eyes open for anyone suspicious, but until we find someone else, he's my number one suspect." He looked at the others.

Emmett nodded agreement and then looked at Joseph. "Sorry."

Joseph forced a smile and nodded. Maddie shrugged her shoulders and nodded in turn.

Joseph unwrapped the reins, released the brake, and started the wagon down the gravel road.

Billy Mac turned to face the road behind them and then lay back in the wagon bed—his arms under his head—and closed his eyes. The summer sun beat down on his face, and he wiped the sweat from the corner of his eyes. *Good Lord. Air's so thick it's hard to breathe.*

"Mackie," Emmett said, "what else was in your backpack?"

"That's just it," Billy Mac said, eyes still closed. "My sketchpad and—"

"Oh, Billy Mac!" Maddie cried from the bench. "Not all of your drawings?"

"Yeah, that's what makes me really mad," Billy Mac answered. "All my sketches for the past year or so. I hate losin' them more'n that stupid pipe." He rolled his head over and looked at Emmett.

Emmett was shaking his head back and forth. "Rats! Wish we could find whoever—"

"Yeah, and what really sets me off," Billy Mac said, cutting him off, "is that I'd made a sketch of that pipe—a pretty good one too! Took me all one afternoon."

Joseph called, "Whoa!" and brought the wagon to a halt. Billy Mac sat up and turned to face the bench. Joseph and Maddie were looking at him.

"You made a sketch of the pipe?" Joseph asked. "Could you do it again from memory?"

"I could make a likeness," Billy Mac answered, "but not of all the detail. When I draw I focus on angles and shading, line thickness and such. I don't focus so much on the overall object."

No one said anything. *All my drawings gone!* Billy Mac shook his head, turned back around, and lay down again. Joseph started the wagon.

"I've got an idea," Emmett said next to him. "I think Joseph's right. The whole mystery surrounds that pipe. There's something about it. We've got to find someone that can tell us more about those ceremonial pipes. Maybe the answer is in what kind of ceremonies they were used at."

"Father didn't really know much about them," Joseph called from the bench without turning around. "That's why he sent us to see Askuwheteau. If we lived closer to the reservation we'd be more involved in the history of our people, but being here in Monticello, we're so far removed that we've never really been involved in the tribal activities. I hate to say so, but that's the way it is. We should know more, but we don't."

"There must be someone we can talk to," Maddie said. "Surely we can—"

"I've got it!" Emmett cried. "We'll go see Ms. Lee at the library!" Emmett said. "She and I are big buddies."

"You think there are books on this kinda thing?" Billy Mac asked.

"Don't know, Mackie." Emmett smiled and hunched his shoulders.

Maddie turned around to face them. "Even if there isn't, she may be able to tell us who to talk to, a historian of some kind. Good idea!" She gave Emmett one of those winsome smiles, and he sat there smiling back.

Billy Mac watched them and shook his head. *Good grief.* "Okay, so we'll go see Ms. Lee after we drop Maddie off and get back to town."

"Oh, no you don't!" Maddie said. "I'm going with you."

"But, Maddie," Joseph started, "I won't be able to bring you back out to the farm tonight or tomorrow. I've too much work to do."

"That's okay," she said. "When we get to the farm, give me two minutes to get my things. I'll just stay with Aunt Charlotte in town. She loves to have me come for visits. She gets so lonely there by herself."

"Good!" agreed Emmett, and he gave Maddie another smile.

Billy Mac just shook his head. *Sheesh!*

Chapter 18

Billy Mac held Henry by the harness while Emmett and Joseph unhooked the wagon. He led the horse into his stall and then slipped the harness off his face. Joseph came in with a bucket of grain and the three boys helped to rub Henry down and brush him. Joseph checked his water, and then Billy Mac and Emmett followed him out and set the latch.

"Thanks, Joseph," Billy Mac said. He followed Emmett toward the street where Maddie waited for them.

"Yeah, thanks, Joseph." Emmett turned and waved.

"See you, guys," he replied. "Let me know what you turn up at the library." He waved and then turned to go into the shop.

Billy Mac and Emmett caught up to Maddie and the three of them headed toward the river. There, on a high bluff overlooking the river, sat the library that the town had built with a grant from Andrew Carnegie.

Billy Mac opened the door, held it for Maddie and Emmett, and then followed them in. The little bell on the doorframe clinked as he closed the door behind him.

Billy Mac could see why Emmett loved coming here. It was always cool and quiet inside the handsome building. He walked over to window and looked down at the river. *I could sit here and sketch all day.*

"Was wondering where you've been keeping yourself, Emmett," a voice called from the back of the room. Billy Mac turned around as a middle-aged woman, graceful and neat, walked from the shadows between two stacks of bookshelves. She smiled at Emmett. "Thought you would have needed to swap out your stack of books last week sometime. Something else keeping you occupied?" She winked at Maddie who gave her a big smile in return.

"Hi, Ms. Lee," Emmett said. "Yeah, I do have several I need to bring back so I can pick out some new ones. Maybe a new Tom Swift."

"Did you bring me a couple of converts?" She nodded at Billy Mac. "I've been after this one for years."

Billy Mac liked Ms. Lee. "I know, I know," he said. He shrugged and smiled at her joke.

"Well, we came for a different reason," Emmett said. He looked over at Billy Mac, who nodded for him to continue.

"Ohhh," Ms. Lee said. "I sense something serious here. Let's go in the back and sit down." She turned and led them to the back of the room. There were two large harvest tables where visitors could sit and read. She pulled out a chair for Maddie at one of the tables. "Here, my dear."

Maddie smiled at her and sat down. Billy Mac and Emmett did the same. The librarian looked at the three of them and folded her hands on the table. "Okay, what's up?" she asked.

"You start, Emmett," Billy Mac said.

Emmett related their findings: the hidden room in the old cabin, the map and the tomahawk pipe, the story Doc Miller had told them about the old Indian treated by his father so many years ago, the tale of the hidden gold, and their first visit to Askuwheteau. Billy Mac finished with his backpack being stolen, the second visit to Askuwheteau, and the Indian's peculiar actions.

"Maddie and Joseph don't suspect Askuwheteau," Billy Mac told her. "Emmo and I . . . well . . . we're not sure. Guess we need to think on it some more." He winced, feeling guilty for suspecting the old man.

"We need to know more about those tomahawk pipes, Ms. Lee," Emmett said. "Joseph and his pa don't really know much about them. All they know is that this could have been some kind of ceremonial pipe. Are there books that can tell us more about the pipes and the different ceremonies they were used for?"

Ms. Lee sat for a moment nodding. She finally spoke. "I had heard stories when I was a little girl of hidden Indian gold but nothing more than that. No details, no specifics—certainly nothing about who might have been involved, such as your family, Maddie. I don't think I ever believed them. Not sure I do even now, despite all of this news you've brought me." She shook her head.

"Why not, Ms. Lee?" asked Maddie.

"Well," she said, "after Tecumseh was killed in Canada the whole effort for those Indians living in Prophetstown just fell apart. Many of them literally starved to death. They would have used any gold they had to feed themselves."

"Exactly what I told them," murmured Maddie. She crossed her arms and slumped down in her chair.

"But we'd still like to learn more about these pipes," Billy Mac said. "Gold or no gold, there's still somethin' mysterious about that pipe we found."

"Oh, yes, I agree with that. It would certainly appear so." She rubbed her chin and thought for a moment. "I can't think of any books that would give you any information on Shawnee or Miami ceremonial pipes, but I can tell you what I know about them. I suppose, like many old-maid librarians, I'm somewhat a local historian," she said with a laugh.

"When Tecumseh and his brother founded Prophetstown, they encouraged other tribes to join them, and at one time members of as many as fourteen other tribes did so. They included the Miami, Wea, Kickapoo, Piankeshaw, Potawatami, Chickamauga, and even Canadian tribes like the Ojibway and Iroquois. Prophetstown stretched for over a mile on the bluffs of the Wabash with a population of over three thousand.

"According to the Prophet, the great spirit Manitou would grant them the power to defeat the whites and reclaim their homelands if they would return to the old ways and reject the whites. Tecumseh and the Prophet proclaimed the whites to be children of the devil. This was a powerful message to thousands of warriors that were angry from being pushed off of their lands.

"By 1808 Tecumseh had a powerful message and he traveled wide to deliver it. At one time he had several thousand warriors at his command throughout the Northwest Territory.

"To those tribes he could not visit in person, Tecumseh sent emissaries. He sent gifts of *wampum* to other tribal leaders, and with them a personal message to come and join them in Prophetstown on the Wabash. If each tribe stood alone, they would fall one by one to the white devils. But standing together would please Moneto and they could drive the whites from their homelands forever.

"However, his message had to be sent in a secret, coded manner in case it was intercepted by white soldiers. Tecumseh was very clever. Along with the gifts of *wampum*, Tecumseh's emissaries presented tomahawk pipes to the other tribal leaders. They were things of beauty with carved and painted handles. If these pipes should fall into the hands of the enemy, they would appear to be nothing more than a common ceremonial pipe. But, to the tribal leaders, the message coded into the carving and painting bore a strong message: Moneto wished for all to gather together at Prophetstown."

Billy Mac was stunned. *No, it can't be!*

Emmett and Maddie looked just as floored.

Maddie sat up straight. "You're telling us the pipe Billy Mac found in that old cabin could have been a pipe like that, one that had a hidden message carved into the handle?"

"Yes." Ms. Lee smiled. "If it was a very ornately carved and painted pipe, it very well could be, given that the old Indian had been a part of Tecumseh's band of warriors. He could have used the same method of secretly passing on an important message."

Billy Mac looked down at the table, looked through it into nothing, shaking his head. "Do you know what you're saying?" he said and looked up.

"I do, Mackie!" Emmett beamed. "That pipe someone stole from you is the map to the buried gold!"

Chapter 19

"Unbelievable!" Joseph's jaw dropped. "I can't believe it!" He wiped his hands with a towel and then wiped the sweat from his face. He untied his leather apron and laid it on the workbench. "Come. Let's go out and sit in the shade for a minute and cool off."

Billy Mac followed Joseph, Emmett, and Maddie out of the shop. Emmett and Maddie sat on the bench under the window. Billy Mac helped Joseph drag another bench from the other side of the doorway and they sat on it.

"Nice out here," Joseph murmured.

"Ma's afraid the well's going to go dry if we don't get some rain," Emmett said. "They've closed down the Strand until it cools off a little."

"Yeah, the hens all stopped layin', it's so hot," Billy Mac said. *That means no egg money.* "And Pa says to be careful 'bout how much water I use on the tomato garden. Gotta use as little as I can to keep 'em alive."

"You ought to see the creek," Maddie said. "Lowest I've ever seen it. Probably halfway down."

No one spoke for a minute. Billy Mac closed his eyes, willing the breeze to blow.

"So what next?" Joseph asked beside him.

Billy Mac opened his eyes, shrugged an "I don't know," and looked at Emmett; he had closed his eyes too and was leaning back against the wall of the shop. Billy Mac looked at Maddie.

"I don't know, either," she said. "We can't go any further without that pipe, right?"

"Right," Emmett said without opening his eyes.

"So that's it?" Billy Mac snapped. "You just gonna quit?" He clenched his jaw and crossed his arms. He could feel his ears turning red.

"Cool down, Mackie," Emmett said calmly. "No one said we were going to quit."

"What do you propose?" Joseph asked. His eyebrows furrowed at the question.

Emmett opened his eyes, sat up, looked at the other three, and smiled, letting the effect of the question linger. "Simple. I propose we get our pipe back."

"Hmph!" Maddie smirked. She tilted her head and brushed the hair out of her eyes. "And just how are we going to do that?"

"Not entirely sure yet," Emmett said. "It's almost supper time now, so we can't do much more today."

Joseph nodded. "And I have to get back to work to finish an order," Joseph said.

"And I promised Aunt Charlotte we'd have dinner together to catch up," Maddie said.

"How 'bout this?" Billy Mac said. "How 'bout in the morning we pack a lunch, walk the tracks out to the farm, maybe jump in the creek and cool off, and make a plan. Would your Ma and Doc care, Maddie?"

"You know they wouldn't," Maddie said. "They like to have you all out. And we won't have to pack a lunch. Ma will take care of us."

"Afraid I can't go," Joseph said. "Too much work to do."

"That's okay, Joseph," Emmett said. "We'll keep you posted."

Billy Mac opened the screen door and walked into his house. Emmett was right behind him. He let the door smack shut on the spring.

"Pa?" Billy Mac called.

"Yes, son?" a distant voice answered.

"Emmett's gonna stay the night, okay?"

"Okay," the voice answered. "There are things in the ice box and tomatoes by the pump. Fix yourselves something to eat. I have to go back down to the jailhouse."

"Okay, thanks!" both boys echoed.

"Oh and, Billy Mac?" his father called again. "I put your sketchbook on the kitchen table. I needed some paper a few days ago. Took it out of your backpack before it came up missing. Sorry I didn't ask first; you weren't around. Forgot about it till a little while ago."

Billy Mac couldn't talk; he was too stunned. He took a deep breath and looked at Emmett who started for the kitchen. Billy Mac followed. There on the kitchen table lay Billy Mac's sketchbook. *Oh, my! I can't believe it.* He picked it up, flipped through the pages, and found what he was looking for: a beautiful, detailed drawing of the missing tomahawk pipe.

Billy Mac lay on top of his sleeping bag on the screened porch. It was another clear night.

After supper he and Emmett had taken the drawing to Joseph's house. Neither he nor his father could make out any of the carvings and symbols.

"Joseph must not have told his pa about Askuwheteau, that we think he was involved with the backpack," Billy Mac said.

"Yeah, guess not," Emmett murmured from his sleeping bag. "Or else his pa wouldn't have suggested that we take it out to him for interpretation."

"So what'll we do?" Billy Mac asked. "There's no one else around here that can do it, is there?"

"Not that I know of, Mackie." Emmett sighed. "I say we go back down to Ms. Lee first thing in the morning and take it to her. Maybe she'll have a suggestion."

Billy Mac looked at the sky. He listened as Emmett's breathing slowed down to a rhythm. It was far enough into the summer that the high chirping of tree frogs drowned out the crickets and cicadas. Their song was constant. *Dang, they're loud. How's he sleepin'?*

"Emmo?" he asked softly. "You asleep?"

"Hmmm?" Emmett grunted. "What?"

"Was wonderin' if you was asleep."

"Reckon not," the older boy replied. "'Sup?"

"You ever think about your pa?" Billy Mac asked.

"Yeah, every now and then," Emmett answered in a sleepy voice. "I have a lot of memories of him. I was ten when he went off to the war. Ma keeps a picture of him on that little table by her bed—you've seen it—so, I reckon she thinks about him every day."

Neither spoke for a minute.

"I remember he was funny, and kind," Emmett said. "Too bad you never knew your ma."

"Yeah," Billy Mac answered. "Sometimes when I look up at the stars I wonder . . . I wonder if she looks down on us. Guess that's goofy, ain't it?"

"I don't know, Mackie," Emmett said. "I think that hoping she does is a good thing, that it helps us to think that your ma and my pa watch out after us every now and then. It's a comforting thought."

"Yeah, I reckon. Night, Emmo."

"'Night, Mackie."

Chapter 20

Billy Mac trailed behind Emmett and Maddie as they walked along the railroad tracks toward the Millers' farm. He looked down at his bare legs. *Not too shabby.* Earlier that morning Emmett had gone home and brought back his mother's sewing scissors. Each had cut off their dungarees at knee level.

Billy Mac was walking on one of the rails, his arms stretched out. *I'm gettin' better and better at this.* He heard Maddie giggle so he paused and looked up.

"Can't remember ever seeing you two in cut-off trousers," Maddie teased without looking around. Neither boy answered. "I must say, you both have pretty legs, but your laced-up boots don't do much for you."

"Aw, c'mon, Maddie," Billy Mac grumbled, concentrating on his balance. "It's just so blamed hot. Hey, Emmo, jump up on that other rail."

"No thanks!" Emmett answered. He took a couple steps back and pushed Billy Mac off with a laugh. "Not getting caught in that trap again." Billy Mac caught himself and stepped in between the tracks to walk with the other two.

"Okay," Maddie said, "tell me the rest of it. What did Ms. Lee say when you showed her the sketch?"

"She was leavin' to catch the train to Lafayette today for some kinda librarian conf'rence," Billy Mac answered. "It's gonna be at Purdue, so she said she'd look up an old professor friend of hers to see if he can help."

"Yeah," Emmett said. "He's an anthropologist, and she said he's also quite the historian on the tribes that were in this area. She thinks he can point us in a good direction for help."

"And you gave her the sketch to take with her?" Maddie asked.

"Yeah." Billy Mac shrugged. "Kinda had to. Didn't have much choice if we wanted her help."

"She promised to be very careful with it," Emmett added.

"When does she get back?" Maddie asked.

"Couple of days," Billy Mac answered. "Said she'd call Pa at the jailhouse and let him know when she was sure." He stepped over the rail to the right hand side of the track to walk in the shade. The sun had baked the grass and the leaves of the smaller bushes into a sweet, parched smell.

"Can't believe it's so hot so early in the morning," Emmett murmured. "Can't wait to jump in the creek."

"It'll be funny to see how much water is left," Maddie said. "Gramps is worried about the corn crop. Said he hasn't seen it this dry since he was a boy."

"Well, as long as there's enough to wallow in and cool off," Billy Mac said. He stepped up on the rail and spread his arms out.

"Looks like you're ready to take off flying, Mackie," Emmett joked.

"Wish I could," Billy Mac said. *I'd fly north for the summer.*

They reached the old cabin and turned off the tracks. The grass was over their heads. They thrashed through it with their arms to make a path. Large, tobacco-spitting grasshoppers flushed out from the onslaught and surfed on the heat waves radiating from the scorched earth. The drone of cicadas was constant.

When they reached the old tree that bridged the creek, Maddie crossed first. Billy Mac followed her, climbed to the top of the limestone cropping, and turned to see Emmett hop off of the tree. Billy Mac sat down and Maddie plopped down next to him. *Nice up here in the shade.*

"Good Lord!" Maddie exclaimed. "Billy Mac, can I have some water?"

Billy Mac shuffled through his backpack and held out the canteen. Maddie cupped her hands and said, "Will you pour a little out for me?"

Billy Mac did so and she splashed the cool water onto her face. "Whew! Better. Hey, where'd you get *that* old backpack?"

Billy Mac took a drink from the canteen and put it back in the bag. "It was my grandpa's from when he was in the army. 'Remember the Maine!' Wish I could find the one that got stole though. Sure would like to have it back."

Emmett climbed up to them, sat down, took his shirt off, made a pillow out of it, and lay down on the rock. "Seems like it's always just a little bit cooler up here on this rock," he said.

Billy lay back and looked up at the trees. The rock felt cool through his shirt. Cottonwood leaves flickered with a soft rustle.

"Okay, I'm better," Maddie said. Billy Mac looked over at her. She stood up and wiped her forehead. "I'm going to walk up to the house to get Boomer. I'll be back in a bit." She walked down off of the boulder.

Emmett sat up. "Want us to go with you, Maddie?"

"No, I'll be right back." She started toward the field.

"You gonna bring you some swimmin' trunks?" Billy Mac called after her.

"Some of them old-fashioned striped ones you see in the picture books?" Emmett added.

"I think not," she called back without stopping or turning around. "And teasing me will lessen your chances of me bringing back some fried chicken."

Both boys smiled and called in unison, "Sorry!"

Billy Mac looked over at Emmett.

"Well, Mackie, what do you think?"

Billy Mac stood up, walked to the ledge of the boulder, and looked down into the creek. "Hey, Emmett, the water's down about six feet. Look at this. There's a little ledge stickin' out down there. Couldn't see it before when the creek was full. It'll make a great little climbin' platform."

Emmett walked up next to him and looked down. "Sure would," he agreed.

"How deep do you reckon it still is down there?" Billy Mac wondered out loud.

"Let's see," Emmett said. He walked down off the boulder, looked around, and picked up a large rock with both hands. He swung his arms toward the creek and let it fly so that it landed in the water straight out from the little ledge. It hit like a cannon ball with a loud, deep kerplunk and sent a tail of water several feet into the air. "Plenty deep! We can still jump in. No diving headfirst though."

"Look, Mackie, straight up." Billy Mac followed Emmett's gaze into the trees lining the creek. "That big branch from the sycamore yonder comes straight overhead. If we can get the rope straight over that branch, it will be perfect. Grab it, will you?"

Billy Mac scurried back to the top of the boulder and dug into the backpack. "Here you go," he said, and he threw a coil of cotton well rope to Emmett.

Emmett sat down. Billy Mac watched him tie a knot at one end of the rope. Then he tied a knot about every twelve inches for several feet. He stood up, recoiled the rope, and held it in his right hand with the loose end still in his left hand. "Here goes nothing," he said. Billy Mac nodded back.

Emmett swung the coiled rope back and forth a few times and then reared back and hurled the coil into the air. "Hmph!" The rope unwound as it circled up and over the sycamore branch, but the weight of the rope pulled it back over so that it all fell to the ground.

"Almost!" Billy Mac cried. "Give it another try!"

Emmett repeated the effort a few times, but five minutes later he slumped down to the ground. "Rats!"

Billy Mac walked down off of the boulder and looked around. He walked over to the fallen tree and grabbed the stub of a branch that was sticking out to one side. He pulled on it several times, and with a final heave broke it loose. "All we need is a little weight on the one end so that when it gets over the branch it won't come sliding back. Here, give me the rope."

Emmett tossed him the coil. On the end without the knots, Billy Mac wrapped the rope around the piece of wood, tied it, and handed the loose end of the rope to Emmett. "Here, hold on to this." He walked off to the side a few steps to gauge his arc, swung his arms a few times for practice, and then with a grunt heaved the coil and stick into the air with both hands. They flew over the sycamore branch, sat still, and then slowly started sliding back until the stick caught.

"Mackie, you're a genius!" Emmett cried.

"Here, hand me your end," Billy Mac said, extending his hand to Emmett without taking his eyes off of the sycamore branch.

Emmett did so, and Billy Mac softly bounced the rope to let the slack work its way over the branch. The weight of the stick dropped it down more and more. Finally, when it was close enough, Billy Mac jumped up, grabbed the stick, and pulled the rope the rest of the way down. He untied the stick and made a noose, through which he poked the knotted end. Then he pulled the length through the noose, cinching the rope securely around the sycamore branch. He turned to Emmett and smiled victoriously.

"Good man, Mackie!" Emmett said and clapped him on the shoulder. "Toss your end down there to that little ledge and let's give it a try!"

Billy Mac sat down and took off his boots and socks; Emmett did the same next to him. He took his shirt off and threw it on the boulder next to Emmett's. Billy Mac walked back to the edge, looked at Emmett, and raised his eyebrows. *Well, go ahead.*

"Geronimo!" the older boy yelled and jumped out from the ledge. He grabbed his knees in midair and hit the water. Kerploom!

A few seconds later, Emmett's head surfaced and he shook the wet hair out of his eyes. "Perfect, Mackie, just perfect." He smiled. He swam to the little rock ledge and pulled himself onto it. He stood up, grabbed the knotted rope, and a few seconds later, Emmett was standing dripping wet next to Billy Mac. He smiled and nodded toward the creek. "Go for it, Mackie!"

Billy Mac took a step back to launch himself when he heard a dog bark. He turned to see Boomer bounding through the corn rows. Maddie was not too far behind him, carrying a picnic basket in the crook of her arm.

Billy Mac lay on the limestone boulder with his hands behind his head, letting the breeze dry him off. He watched Maddie pick up the tablecloth. She snapped it in the breeze to shake crumbs off, folded it, and stuffed it into the basket with the leftovers. She looked around, brushed the hair out of her eyes, and squinted as she looked off across the field. "Anyone seen Boomer?" Maddie asked.

Billy Mac propped himself up on an elbow. "Uh, yeah. There he is." He pointed a little ways down the tree line where the creek made a sharp bend. Boomer came out of the shadows of the trees, sniffing the ground, and then turned into some brush. "Looks like he's after a rabbit or somethin."

"Sure has been a good day, Maddie," Emmett said. He was lying back with his eyes closed. "The creek felt great, and your ma's chicken is always so good."

"Yeah, Maddie," Billy Mac echoed. "Thanks, and tell your ma thanks too."

"I will," she said absently. She clapped her hands a few times, yelled for Boomer, and then turned back to the boys.

"So what's the plan? There's not much to do until Ms. Lee gets back, right?"

"Right," Emmett said, and he sat up. He rubbed his eyes. "We should get going though, Mackie. I've got a few chores to do before dinnertime."

Billy Mac pulled on his socks, boots, and shirt. Emmett did the same.

There was a sudden barking in the distance from the creek bend and then snarling and snapping as if Boomer was fighting with an animal. The three friends jumped up.

"What the . . . ,"Billy Mac started. He was cut off by a yelp of pain and the sound of a large splash.

"Boomer!" Maddie yelled and started running toward the sounds.

"Maddie, wait!" Emmett called after her. "Wait!"

"Jeezus!" Billy Mac cried and jumped down off the boulder.

He started to follow Maddie and Emmett but stopped to pick up the large stick he had used with the rope. He ran to catch up. They all ran to the bend in the creek where they had seen Boomer sniffing through the brush.

"Boomer!" Maddie called. "C'mere, boy! Boomer!"

"C'mon, Boomer. C'mon!" Billy Mac yelled, and then he whistled short bursts and clapped his hands.

"There he is!" Emmett yelled. He was pointing a little further down the creek bank. Boomer trotted out of the brush toward them. "Here, boy!"

They all bent down. Maddie hugged him around the neck, and Billy Mac rubbed Boomer between his ears. Boomer's tail wagged at the attention.

"Check him out," Emmett said. "Make sure he's not hurt."

Billy Mac rubbed his hands over Boomer's back and turned him around.

Maddie gently pushed Boomer down to the ground and rolled him over. "Looks like he's fine. Gosh, he sure had me scared!" Boomer jumped back to his feet and Maddie hugged him around the neck again.

"Hey," Billy Mac said, "let's go see what the fuss was about." He started walking toward the creek bank where Boomer had come from.

"Wait up, Mackie!" Emmett called. "Might be a raccoon or something."

Boomer ran ahead of them, straight back through the brush. The three of them followed, thrashing their way through the scrub until they came to a little clearing by the creek bank.

"Oh, my gosh!" Maddie cried and put her hands up to her mouth.

"Jeez!" Billy Mac choked. *Would you look at that?!*

A circle of rocks framed the charred, cold remains of a small campfire. A tin plate, fork, and knife lay to one side. A log had been rolled close by to sit on. On the top of the log was a felt hat with a wide, flat brim. A feather stuck out of the hatband.

"Unbelievable," Emmett murmured. He walked over and picked up the hat. "Ever seen this before?" He tossed it to Billy Mac.

"Couldn't swear it's the same one but it looks like the one we saw out at Askuwheteau's cabin, don't it?" Billy Mac said.

"Do you think he—anyone—is still here?" Maddie asked, looking around.

"Don't think so," Emmett said. "Sounded like whoever it was jumped into the creek after Boomer got after him."

Billy Mac walked over to the creek bank and looked down and then across to the other side. *Nothing. Probably long gone by now.* He turned and walked back to the circle of rocks.

Boomer was sniffing around in the sage grass outside of the campsite. Maddie walked over to him and then stopped. "Oh, my gosh!" she cried again.

Billy Mac watched as she bent down in the tall grass. When she stood up, she was holding his stolen backpack. She looked at the boys, speechless.

"Unbelievable!" Emmett exclaimed.

"Wow!" Billy Mac cried and ran over to her. "Oh, Maddie!" She handed him the backpack. He carried it back into the open ground of the campsite and dumped the contents onto the ground. Two cans of beans fell out along with his drawing pencils and the old map they had found several weeks ago in the cabin.

Billy Mac looked up at the other two standing over him. "No pipe."

"Rats!" Emmett swore and walked over to the creek bank.

"Still glad I got this back though," Billy Mac said while holding up the backpack. "Thanks, Maddie."

Maddie smiled at him and then frowned. "It's eerie to think that all the time we were eating and you two were swimming someone was sitting over here," she said.

"Yeah, I know what you mean," Billy Mac answered. He walked over to the creek bank, stood next to Emmett, and looked across the creek into the shadows of the cottonwoods and sycamores. *Are you over there? Are you watching us—again?*

"Okay," Emmett said. "Let's go get our stuff and get back to town."

"Right," Billy Mac countered. "Let's go." He walked over, put the small pile into his backpack, and then walked over and picked up the tin plate, knife, and fork. He hesitated and then put them in the pack as well. He tossed the felt hat to Emmett. "Here, Emmo. You keep this."

"C'mon, boy." Maddie clapped after Boomer and they started back toward the limestone boulder.

"Just one thing though," Maddie said to the boys. "I'm going back to town with you, and I'm taking Boomer with me. Help me carry the basket up to the house so I can get a few things and tell Ma."

Billy Mac looked at her and nodded and then looked at Emmett.

"Sure, Maddie, sure," Emmett said and smiled at Billy Mac.

Good grief.

Chapter 21

Billy Mac didn't see Emmett for a few days. His mother was taking advantage of the Strand being closed due to the heat and kept Emmett busy at the theater with odds and ends that needed fixing.

Billy Mac worked in the garden, kept Morris's Market stocked with tomatoes, and did some sketching. There was not a lot to do since the hens weren't laying.

On the third day Billy Mac's father got a call from Lafayette. Ms. Lee would be on the late afternoon train and would meet them at the library. At the appropriate time, he pulled Emmett away from the Strand, gathered Maddie from her Aunt Charlotte's, and called on Joseph just as he was closing shop.

Billy Mac stood with the others and looked up the sidewalk that led to the Skinners' house.

"Next time you go out to Maddie's for a picnic, I'm coming too," Joseph said. "Can't believe I missed all the excitement!"

"Yeah, it was something," Billy Mac answered. "Never a dull moment. Emmo, let me see that note from Ms. Lee again."

Emmett handed Billy Mac the paper they had found taped to the window of the locked library door. Billy Mac unfolded it and read it again. It said: "E. Trentham & Company—Meet me at the home of Mr. & Mrs. Skinner. M. Lee, 6.00 p.m."

"Well," Emmett said over Billy Mac's shoulder, "not sure what this means, but let's go." Maddie, Joseph, and Billy Mac followed him up the walk and up the steps of the porch.

Billy Mac knocked. He could hear footsteps and a second later the door opened. There stood Principal Skinner.

"Yes, yes," he said with a smile. "Remarkable, just remarkable. Come in, come in," he said and ushered them inside.

One by one they shuffled in silently and stood in the foyer. "This way, this way," Skinner said and opened a door into a parlor. *Does he always say everything twice?*

Ms. Lee was sitting at a table with a smile on her face. "Hello, you three." She looked at Joseph. "Hello, Joseph. Are you a part of this mystery, too?"

"Hello, Ms. Lee," he answered with his flashing smile. "On occasion." He nodded.

Billy Mac fidgeted. Beside him, Emmett couldn't contain himself. "Ms. Lee . . . ," he started, working his hands as if juggling, pleading for some answers.

"Okay." She smiled. "Why don't you all find a spot and sit down?"

"Yes, yes," Mr. Skinner agreed. "Please sit."

Once seated, Ms. Lee began. "Earlier today I saw my friend at Purdue, Dr. Thompson," she said. "First, he was impressed with the quality and detail of the drawing—a compliment to you, Billy Mac." She nodded at the boy.

"Thanks," Billy Mac said. "But could he tell you anything? Could he read the carvings?"

"No, unfortunately not," she said.

Billy Mac shook his head and snorted. *Jeez! I knew it.* The other three teenagers let out a collective groan.

"But," she said, "he knew of someone that can!" She looked up at Principal Skinner who stood, smiling, beside her chair.

"I confess," he said, "to being quite the authority on our aboriginal brethren, with an ardent concentration on those of resident heritage."

Billy Mac looked at him quizzically. Maddie and Joseph looked equally bewildered. Billy Mac turned to Emmett who said with a smile, "He's an expert on the local Indian tribes!" Emmett then looked at the principal. "Can you interpret the carvings on the pipe, Mr. Skinner?"

"Well, yes and no, my boy," the man replied. "I most certainly can for the portion of the portrayed representation, however, I fear that only reveals one half of the message conveyed."

"But what does it say, sir?" Maddie interjected.

"It says, Ms. Miller, 'the secret lies in the mouth of.'" Then he stopped talking.

"The secret lies in the mouth of what?" Billy Mac asked.

"I don't know, young man," Mr. Skinner replied. "That is all the representation reveals. The other side of the pipe would convey the balance of the message."

From the hallway came the sound of the front door being opened. A moment later it slammed shut, followed by the sound of footsteps.

"Alfred?" a woman yelled. "Are you home? Where in the blazes are you? Alfred?!"

Billy Mac looked at Skinner. His face had gone ashen and his features drooped.

"Yes, dear, in the parlor," he called.

Mrs. Skinner charged into the room, the front of her dress wet. She looked at the teenagers and then focused on Joseph. "And what, may I ask, are *you* doing here?"

Ms. Lee rose from her chair and took a step forward. "They came with me to solicit the help of your husband on a bit of local history," she said.

"And, you are?" Mrs. Skinner countered, her eyes squinted.

"Matilda Lee, local librarian. How do you do?"

"Hmph!" The principal's wife looked at her husband. "Do you know what those little hellions did to me this time? Well, do you?" she demanded.

"Why, no my dear," he answered.

"They-they . . . oh!" She threw up her hands, turned, and marched out of the room. As she stomped down the hall her voice faded. "Why I don't pack up and leave this godforsaken town is beyond me."

"And me," Billy Mac heard Mr. Skinner murmur to himself. He then turned to his guests. "I must apologize for the rudeness of my wife. It seems there is a faction intent on making my wife's existence rather miserable." He paused then added, "If they were of proper age, I believe I would buy them a drink!" He winked at Billy Mac.

Chapter 22

Billy Mac sat with Maddie, Emmett, and Joseph on the benches outside the blacksmith shop. Boomer was lying in the cool of the dirt by the tree trunk.

"The secret lies in the mouth of," Emmett repeated for the third time.

"Well," Billy Mac said, "now we know why I kept seeing things—or someone. Whoever or whatever it was must know about the secret and is lookin' for it too."

"What do you mean, whoever or whatever? You still think there's a ghost out there, Mackie? You saw that campsite. Ghosts don't build campfires and cook."

"Yeah, I know. Just thinkin' out loud."

"I know every part of that farm and most of the property around us," Maddie said. "In the mouth of what?"

"Some of those cottonwoods and sycamores by the creek are huge," Emmett said. "Could the gold have been hid inside one or more of them? A big hollow spot inside a trunk could be the 'mouth.'"

"Some of those cottonwoods are old enough to have been there a hundred years ago," Joseph said. "It would have to stand out more than the others in order to be a landmark."

"None come to mind." Maddie shook her head back and forth.

"I don't think they would have hollowed out a tree though," Billy Mac said. "From the way the story goes, they would've had to hide it fast."

"What about the well on the farm?" Emmett asked. "Could that be what they meant?"

"No," Maddie said. "They had to hide the gold long before a well was ever dug on the farm. That can't be it." A moment later she added, "I still don't think there is any buried gold, but this sure is a mystery."

"So what do we do now?" Billy Mac asked.

"Well," Emmett said, "we have to do a few things. We have to keep working our way around to see if anything stands out." He sat quiet for a moment and rubbed his chin. "And we need to keep a lookout to see if the mystery man shows up again."

"Do you really think it is Askuwheteau?" Joseph said. "I still don't believe he's a thief or a liar."

"I know, Joseph," Emmett said, "but right now he's the only clue we have. At the very least, he knows more than he's telling us."

"I have to agree with that," Maddie said. "I like that old man and I don't think he's guilty, but he does know something he's not sharing."

"So what do we do?" Billy Mac repeated.

"I think tomorrow morning Mackie and I pack up some gear and supplies and camp out until we find something," Emmett said. "Joseph, you can come out and help whenever you can get away from the shop."

Joseph nodded agreement. "I can probably get out there a few hours every evening or so. Where will you set up camp?"

"Right there by Maddie's limestone boulder. The tree bridges the creek there so we can easily scout around on both sides. Plus, we have the rope there, and we can hop in every now and then for a quick swim to get away from this heat!"

"And," Maddie added, "if you camp there, Boomer and I can come down and help until it gets late. If you walk me back to the house at night, you can keep Boomer at the camp with you. That way you won't have to worry about anyone sneaking around; he'd flush them out."

"Good idea," Billy Mac said. He reached down to rub between Boomer's ears; the dog's tail thumped the hard ground.

"Uh, oh," Joseph said.

Billy Mac followed Joseph's gaze and looked toward the street. Gus and his band of followers were heading their way.

"Hey, guys," Joseph called.

"Hey, Joseph," Gus murmured, a lopsided frown on his face.

"What's up?" Billy Mac asked. "What's the problem?"

Gus dug his hands into his overalls. "That Skinner woman. We're in trouble again." The other boys shuffled nervously behind Gus.

"We heard there was some kind of problem. What happened?" Emmett asked.

"That's just it; we didn't do nothin'!" Gus cried. "It warn't our fault!"

"But what happened?" Emmett repeated.

"We decided we'd try again to make friends with her since school's startin' so soon," Gus said. "We thought we'd take her somethin' nice."

"Like a peace offering?" Joseph asked. Billy Mac could tell Joseph was trying hard not to laugh.

"Yeah, a peace offering!" Gus replied.

"Well?" Billy Mac asked.

"Well, we thought and thought of our favorite thing," Gus said. "Somethin' nobody else had. We decided we'd give 'er my jumper."

"Your jumper?" Maddie asked, her eye brows furrowed.

"Yeah, my jumper," Gus answered. "He ain't never lost. He's the best I ever had. Never be another one like him. So we put him in a cigar box with some grass and a little water, and when we saw her walking home, we ran up to give it to her."

"Oh, my!" Maddie put her hand up to her mouth. "You gave her a frog?"

"Weren't just no frog—he was the best ever!" Gus said. "He ain't never lost!" The boys behind him murmured, "That's right. He's the best."

"So what happened?" Emmett asked again.

"We walked up to her on the sidewalk and told her how sorry we was about everything that's happened and that we wanted to give her something special," Gus said. "She said something nasty about 'why should she want a old cigar box' in a mean kinda way, and then she opened it."

"And?" Billy Mac asked.

"Well, he jumped out of the box," Gus said. "Landed right about here." He patted his chest. "Just about where her—"

"We get it." Emmett cut him off. "What happened?"

"Well, he plum skeared her and she grabbed 'im and musta squeezed 'im too hard," Gus said.

"And?" Billy Mac echoed.

"And he peed on her!" Gus exclaimed.

Maddie put her hand to her mouth again. "Oh, my gosh!" she gasped. "He peed on her?"

"Yeah!" Gus said. "She shouldn't a squeezed 'im so hard! It warn't our fault!"

Billy Mac, Emmett, and Joseph busted out laughing.

"It ain't funny! We're gonna get it again. He peed all over her, and it warn't our fault!"

Billy Mac laughed so hard he couldn't talk, but Emmett held his hands up in protest.

"I know, I know, sorry. What happened after that?"

"Well, she was so mad," Gus said. "She threw my jumper over the bluff; we ain't never gonna be able to get him back. I lost the best jumper I ever had, and we're gonna get it from her too. What can we do, Emmett?" He hung his head and dug his hands deeper into his overalls.

"Well," Emmett answered, "there's no doubt you boys are going to catch it from her all during school—if she stays here."

Uh, oh. Billy Mac stopped laughing and looked at Emmett. *What're you doin', Emmo?*

Gus looked up. "What'dya mean, 'if she stays here'?"

Emmett shrugged. "If something doesn't change. I mean, everyone knows she hates it here. I'm saying if she doesn't start liking it, I think she'd go back to Lafayette—and leave Monticello forever."

"You reckon?"

"Sure. If things don't change," Emmett answered. "Even Mr. Skinner himself said she hates living here. And I heard her say myself that she doesn't know why she doesn't pack up and leave."

"What about Mr. Skinner? He'd go too?"

"I don't think so. I think he'd stay," Emmett said. "Just my hunch, but I think he likes it here and would be happy. And he's a nice enough guy."

"So . . . ," Gus started.

"Things just don't need to change," Emmett said. "She needs to stay mad as a hornet."

Gus narrowed his eyes and nodded. "Thanks, Emmett. C'mon, guys."

Billy Mac watched the boys clamor together, talking over plans as they walked down the sidewalk and turned down the street. Emmett and Joseph howled. Maddie had tears running down her face.

"Oh, my gosh," Maddie repeated, trying to catch her breath. "It peed on her!" They all busted out again.

Chapter 23

Billy Mac unrolled his sleeping bag inside of the pup tent he had set up and then crawled out. He looked over to see how Emmett was doing inside his rig and then walked over to the creek bank and looked down.

"Gosh, Emmo," Billy Mac called, "I can't believe it. The creek's just about dried up. It's only been a few days since we were swimmin'." *No more dips for us now.*

"Yeah," Emmett answered from inside his tent. "Sure went down fast. Guess all the little creeks that feed into it have all dried up. So much for our cooling off now and then."

"Nothing left but a big pool of water down there in that one deep spot," Billy Mac said. "I can see dry creek bed pokin' through, up and down both ways." He wiped the sweat from his forehead. "Couple more days and we'll be able to just walk up and down in it."

A dog barked and Billy Mac turned to look for Boomer. He couldn't see the dog through the tall cornstalks, but he could hear him loping through them. Boomer eventually shot out of the end of a row. Maddie and Joseph followed a minute later.

Boomer ran up, Billy Mac rubbed him between the ears, and then the dog took off to scout the creek bank.

"Hey, guys!" Joseph called. Billy Mac waved back as Emmett crawled out of his tent.

Maddie walked up and set her picnic basket on the ground. "All set up?" Maddie asked.

"Yep," Billy Mac answered, eyeing the picnic basket. "Whatcha got, Maddie?"

"Sandwiches." She smiled. "And some rhubarb pie. Cut 'em fresh this morning. And there's one chicken leg left from last night." She smiled at Emmett.

Billy Mac looked at them looking at each other. *Sheash!* "Well," he said, "we can't work on an empty stomach. Let's eat!"

Billy Mac sat on the top of the boulder with Joseph. Emmett and Maddie sat next to each other further down, closer to the edge.

The sun had set and the first few stars had come out. Billy Mac lay back on the cool rock with his hands behind his head. Cicadas sang in the trees; their tone rose and then fell with the soft breeze as it rustled through the branches.

"What's the plan for tomorrow?" Maddie asked without turning around.

"Not sure," Billy Mac said. "Emmo?"

"Oh, we'll get up and eat—Ma packed us some biscuits—then we'll scout up and down the creek," Emmett said. "We'll try this side first. If we don't see anything, we'll come back and try the other side in the afternoon."

"I have a better idea," Maddie said. "First, you and Billy Mac come up to the house for a good breakfast. Bacon and eggs will do you better than cold biscuits. And you can wash up too. Then Boomer and I will come with you."

"That would be great. Thanks, Maddie," Billy Mac said, sitting up. "I've had Mrs. Trentham's biscuits before. No offense, Emmo."

"None taken," Emmett said. "I've had 'em too!"

"I better get going," Joseph said. "It'll be late before I get back, and I'll have to unhook the wagon and put Henry up." He stood up, stretched, and then walked down off of the boulder.

"Maddie, I'll walk with you and Boomer up to the house. See you guys tomorrow evening," he said and turned toward the cornfield.

"See you, Joseph." Billy Mac waved.

"Yeah, see you, Joseph," Emmett called.

Maddie stood up. "You all want to keep Boomer with you tonight?"

"No, we'll be okay," Emmett said. "You keep him with you."

She gave Emmett a long smile. "Okay," she said. "See you guys for breakfast."

Good grief. "Night, Maddie," Billy Mac said.

She walked down off the boulder and caught up with Joseph, who was waiting at the end of the corn rows. Boomer bounded after them.

It was too hot to sleep in the tents. Billy Mac lay on his sleeping bag on a grassy spot next to the creek bank. Emmett did the same next to him.

A million stars and the Milky Way lit up the sky along with a half moon. Crickets, cicadas, and tree frogs countered each other in cadence.

"What're you thinking, Emmo?" Billy Mac asked.

"Thinking about whoever stole your pipe. He had to steal it for a reason. He had to know there was something special about it, right? Or else, why do it?"

"I think so too," Billy Mac answered. "Much as I hate to, I keep comin' back to Askuwheteau. Nothin' else makes sense."

"Agreed. So you think it was him you saw that first day at the old cabin down by the tracks?"

"Coulda been," Billy Mac said. "Person I saw was wearin' a hat like the one we found at that campsite down the creek yonder."

"No more ghosts then, huh?"

"Don't look that way," Billy Mac answered. *Sure seemed like it at the time though.*

"So if you stole the pipe and you knew about the gold and you put two and two together, what would you do?" Emmett asked. "If you could interpret all the carvings on the pipe and knew where to look, you'd have found it by now, right?"

"Right," Billy Mac agreed.

"And," Emmett continued, "you wouldn't still be hanging around camping by the creek. You'd be long gone, right?"

"Right," Billy Mac echoed.

"So he's still looking. He hasn't found it yet," Emmett concluded.

"Don't look that way," Billy Mac said again.

"That means either he can't interpret the pipe and hasn't found anyone else that can or he still hasn't found the spot that the pipe is pointing to," Emmett said.

Yeah, that makes sense. Hey, a falling star!

"If you were still looking," Emmett continued, "and your campsite had been found out, would you keep looking in the daytime or would you hole up during the day and poke around at night?"

Uh, oh. "Don't know, Emmo. You might," Billy Mac said. He sat up and looked over at Emmett. "What're you thinkin'?"

"Are you tired?" Emmett asked. He sat up.

"Not really, why?"

"Let's go look around a little," Emmett said. "It might give us the advantage. If someone's out there poking around a little, they probably won't think someone else will be too. They'll be off their guard, so to speak. Look." Emmett pointed across the creek. "The angle of the moon keeps us in the dark on this side. The other side is lit up. If someone is out there, he might be sticking to the other side of the creek; he might not want to come back to this side where he tangled with Boomer. It would make it easier for us to see him than for him to see us."

"Makes sense," Billy Mac agreed. "What'dya think? Which way do you want to go?"

"Well, he made camp that way." Emmett pointed off to the right. "We know that. So he's probably checked out that direction pretty good. Let's go that way." He pointed off to the left. "C'mon."

The boys hugged the edge of the creek, careful to stay in the shadows. Billy Mac allowed Emmett to go first, and then he followed, working from tree to tree as they studied the far side of the creek. An hour passed and then another. Billy Mac slipped up next to Emmett, who had squatted behind the trunk of a large oak tree.

"Let's give it up for tonight, Emmo," Billy Mac whispered. "I'm gettin' tired and it's gettin' late."

Emmett stood up and yawned. "Yeah, I could go for that. Morning will come early. Let's—"

A branch snapped across the creek. Billy Mac stooped down and peeked around the side of the tree.

Nothing. "What'dya think?" Billy Mac whispered. "Coulda just been an animal—maybe a deer?"

"Deer don't walk around at night. You know that," Emmett whispered back. He was peering around the other side of the tree. "Cows and horses don't either. Besides, that's not farm land on that side; the train tracks are too close. Hey, look!"

The silhouette of a man slipped from one shadow to another. He wore a wide-brimmed hat with a feather sticking out of it.

"Well, well, guess he had another hat," Emmett said. "Reckon I don't have to give the other one back."

A few minutes went by, and then Billy Mac saw the figure move on down the bank.

"C'mon, Mackie. Let's keep up with him."

Emmett slipped to the next tree. A few seconds later, Billy Mac followed. They went to the next tree and the next, careful to keep to the shadows.

"He's definitely lookin' for something," Billy Mac whispered. "Looks like he's in the same boat as us."

"Mackie!" Emmett was pointing across the creek but back in the direction from which they had come. "Look!"

Billy Mac squinted and tried to focus in the darkness. Then he saw it. Another figure was working its way down the creek, not being as careful as the first.

"Jeezus!" Billy Mac whispered. "What'dya think he's—hey, Emmo! He's following the first guy!"

"Yeah," Emmett whispered back. "And this one's not wearing a hat. Can't tell anything else about him though. Can't get a clear look at him. Rats!"

Billy Mac watched the second figure until he was out of site.

"Jeez, Emmo," Billy Mac said. "Maybe we still got us a ghost after all! Maybe the guy we flushed from that campsite is followin' the old Indian ghost, hoping he'll lead him to the gold!"

"Calm down, Mackie," Emmett said. "Let me think for a minute." A moment later he said, "We've got to get over there. C'mon. Follow me."

"Are you crazy?" Billy Mac whispered. "We ain't gonna go followin' ghosts and who knows what else around in the middle of the night!"

"Mackie, look, we'll stay far behind both of them. We'll just go a little ways, and then we'll cut up to the railroad tracks, head back to the old cabin, cross the creek, and call it a night. Now, come on. We have to get across this creek bed. Look, it's dry down there at this point."

Billy Mac watched Emmett slowly work his way over the creek bank. He reluctantly followed, careful not to step on sticks or make noise. *How does he talk me into these things?*

The creek bed smelled of damp and rot. Billy Mac followed Emmett as the older boy worked his way along the other side, feeling for a place they could scramble up.

"Here we go!" Emmett whispered back to him. Billy Mac watched Emmett grab a large grapevine hanging down. He half-pulled and half-walked up the embankment and then disappeared over the edge. Billy Mac grabbed the grapevine with both hands, tested his weight with it, and then slowly followed up and over.

Once on top, it was easier going. The moon lit the way on this side better. Emmett was moving quickly from tree to tree in front of him. Billy Mac hurried to catch up, crouching to stay out of sight as much as possible.

Five minutes later, Billy Mac watched Emmett stop behind a tree and stoop down. Billy Mac caught up and stooped beside him.

"Let's hold up a minute, Mackie," Emmett whispered.

The ground was soaking wet with dew. Billy Mac wiped his hands on his dungarees.

"We should be close," Emmett whispered. "He should be here somewhere."

There was a rush of movement behind him. Billy Mac started to turn but someone grabbed him from behind and pushed him over the edge of the bank. "Whoa!"

Billy Mac landed in the creek bed on his left shoulder with the wind knocked out of him. "Em," he gasped, trying to catch his breath. He rolled over and dry heaved a few times until he was able to inhale. "Emmo!" he called. He heard scuffling, and then someone crashed off through the brush. "Emmo!"

Billy Mac tried to sit up but his left arm wasn't working. Pain shot through his shoulder, and he cradled his left arm with his right.

"Emmo!"

"Yeah, okay." Emmett's voice sounded shaky. "I'm okay. You all right?"

"Not sure, think I busted my arm," Billy Mac called up to him. "Hold on."

Billy Mac worked his way back along the creek bed until he found some old tree roots that made a crude ladder. With his right arm, he pulled himself up one step at a time and then circled back. He found Emmett sitting with his head in his hands.

"Emmo, you—Jeezus! You're bleedin'!" Billy Mac cried.

"Yeah," Emmett replied. "He busted my head against the tree. Help me up."

Billy Mac reached down with his good arm and helped his friend to stand up. "You gonna be able to walk?"

"Yeah, just give me a minute," Emmett answered. "Just a little woozy." He took a couple deep breaths. "That's better. Let's look at you."

"Can move it a little now, but it hurts like the devil when I do." Billy Mac winced. *Criminy!*

"Take your shirt off and we'll make a sling," Emmett said. "No, here, let me take mine off. Hold your arm and try not to move it."

Emmett pulled his shirt off over his head and spun it a few times, making a long, padded wrap. He carefully tied it around Billy Mac's neck and then tucked the bad arm into the pouch. "Good?" he asked.

"Better," Billy Mac answered. "Your face looks bad."

"Feels like it too," Emmett answered. "C'mon. The train tracks have to be up this way. We'll follow them back to the cabin and cross there. It'll be close to breakfast by the time we get back. We can get Doc to check us out."

Billy Mac followed Emmett through the tall grass.

"Next time Maddie offers us Boomer, I say we take her up on it," Billy Mac murmured.

"Yeah, next time," Emmett grumbled. "Rats! My head hurts!"

Chapter 24

Billy Mac sat with Emmett and Maddie at the kitchen table. He watched Mrs. Miller as she scurried around the room. The smell of bacon, eggs, and flapjacks hung heavy in the air.

"Sure smells good, ma'am," Billy Mac said. He winced as Doc Miller raised his arm to put it in the proper sling he had fashioned for the boy.

"Well, you won't be using this arm to eat with—or anything else—for a few days. You got lucky. A dislocated shoulder will only keep it out of commission for a few days. A break would have been a long healing process. Funny, though, a separation hurts more than a clean break."

"I believe it." The boy winced again.

"I swear!" cried Mrs. Miller. She turned from the sink to face the table and wiped her hands with her apron. "You boys have got to be more careful—wrestling around with each other and falling into the creek bed like that. With all that horseplay, you could have broken your necks, or worse!"

"Yes, ma'am," Emmett replied with a smile.

Doc had butterflied the gash in Emmett's scalp. A large, deep bruise had come out, covering half of his forehead. He had a lopsided grin on his face. Maddie leaned into the table, tilted her head a little, and flicked her hair to the side. "And what was it again that your face battled with?" she asked Emmett.

"Well," he started, "when Mackie and I were leg wrestling, we threw each other over the edge of the bank. He landed in the bottom of the creek bed on his shoulder, and I landed on my face, right onto this big branch that was lying on the bottom."

"Hmph!" Maddie grunted. She crossed her arms, pursed her lips, and squinted a "yeah, right" at both of them.

"Okay," Doc Miller said. He gave Billy Mac a soft pat on the back and stood up. "Not much more I can do for either of you. You're both going to be very sore for a few days. Doctor's orders are plenty of rest and no goofing around. Got it?"

"Yes, sir," Emmett answered.

"Thanks, Doc," Billy Mac said. "Thanks a ton!"

"All right." Mrs. Miller set dishes in front of each of them. "Enough lecturing. You all eat, and then you can rest up some. Wish I had some coffee but it's just too stinking hot to make any. Now eat up!"

"Thank you, ma'am!" Billy Mac and Emmett echoed.

Billy Mac reached for the syrup pitcher with his good hand. *Bet our ghost-man ain't eatin' this good!*

The three friends hung out most of the day in the shade of the tree-lined creek. Billy Mac stayed fairly put and stationary since every movement hurt. He watched Emmett play fetch with Boomer, while Maddie scolded both boys. Joseph showed up at supper time and found them sitting on the limestone ledge overlooking the creek bed. It didn't take long to bring him up to speed with the events of the night.

"He sure got a good piece of both of you!" Joseph said, shaking his head.

"Still can't believe you'd go off in the middle of the night following someone like that," Maddie chastised. "You didn't know who it was. He could have had a gun or a knife. Stupid, just plain stupid!"

"Aw, Maddie," Billy Mac said. "We weren't gonna confront 'em. We just wanted to see who they were and what they were lookin' for."

"Yeah," Emmett agreed. "I don't know how we got in front of the one. We thought we were behind both of them. Whoever got us must have circled around. Beats me how he figured out we were back there."

"But why don't we tell Billy Mac's father?" Maddie demanded. "The sheriff should know that someone is out here running around, someone that's dangerous. He needs to know."

"Mainly because we don't know who it was," Emmett said. "He pushed Mackie over the side of the creek, so Mackie didn't see him. He got hold of me from the back; I never saw him. I don't know that he meant to hurt me so bad. It was just dumb luck that when he threw me aside I fell into that tree. I think he just meant to scare us so we wouldn't go sneaking around looking for him anymore. He did whisper to me for us to 'stay out of it.'"

"I'm think Emmett's right, Maddie," Joseph said. "There's always drifters hoppin' on and off the trains. They're mostly harmless and keep to themselves. The sheriff can't go searching up and down the tracks arresting everyone he finds camping along beside it."

"We'll tell Pa," Billy Mac said, "but not until we can actually find out more about him—who he is, where he's campin', and other stuff. Once we find out, we'll fetch Pa."

"Well, let's talk about that," Maddie said. "First, you saw someone walking slowly down the far side of the bank, and then about fifty yards back you saw another person following him—or it. Right?"

"Right," Emmett said. "The first person was wearing a hat like the one we found at that campsite. The second person was not. But that's all we could tell about either one of them. We could really only see silhouettes."

"Do you think . . . ," Joseph started and then hesitated. "Do you think it was Askuwheteau that you wrestled with?"

Billy Mac had been asking himself the same question since last night. *It just don't add up.* He looked over at Emmett.

"I don't think so," the older boy said. "There are so many different parts to that question."

"Yeah." Billy Mac cut him off. "We all agree he knows somethin' he's not sharin' with us. We all agree he was purposely tryin' to get rid of us that last time we went to his cabin."

"But," Emmett said, "it doesn't make sense that whoever Boomer scuffled with could have been him. Boomer knew Askuwheteau, and they appeared to be friendly with each other when we went out to visit him both times. So I don't think that person camping by the creek could have been Askuwheteau."

"And," Billy Mac added, "the person that attacked us last night rushed up behind us quickly, faster than I think Askuwheteau can probably move. And the person was stronger than I think Askuwheteau could be."

"Plus . . ." Emmett looked down and kicked at a small rock. "I just don't think Askuwheteau would attack us like that. Whoever it was could probably see us well enough to recognize us."

"Agreed," said Joseph. "It sure is a mystery. So what will you do now?"

"You heard what Gramps said," Maddie warned. "No horsing around for a few days."

"Agreed," Emmett said. "Nothing for a few days."

"Yeah, need to heal up a little," Billy Mac agreed.

"We'll ride back to town with you tonight, Joseph," Emmett said. "I think we'll have to be out here longer than I initially thought, and we can't keep imposing on the good graces of Mrs. Miller. So in a couple of days, we'll put more supplies together and come back out. We'll need some food we can put in backpacks, in case we find something somewhere and need to stake it out."

"Yeah," Billy Mac said. "In a few days we can start poking around again. It won't hurt us to walk up and down the creek a little during the daytime, especially if we have Boomer." The dog heard his name and bounded over to Billy Mac. He reached over with his good hand and rubbed the dog between the ears.

"Okay." Maddie gave in. "But can we agree that we'll take it slow and easy—no taking chances?"

"Yeah," Emmett answered. "Fine with me." He gingerly touched his forehead and winced.

"Sure, Maddie," Billy Mac agreed.

"And I'm going to town with you too," Maddie said and stood up. "Might as well get going." She clapped her hands. "C'mon, Boomer!"

Billy Mac trailed the others as they started toward the cornfield. He stopped, looked back across the creek, and clenched his jaw. *Are you over there? Are you watching us? We'll be back.* He turned and followed the others as they slipped between the tall rows of cornstalks.

Chapter 25

Billy Mac finished stowing supplies in his pup tent and, still squatting, duck walked out. It was hard to keep his balance with one arm in a sling. Out in the open, he stood up, brushed himself off with his right hand, stretched, and worked his bad shoulder up and down a few times. He glanced over to see Emmett on all fours backing out of his tent.

"Nice to rest up for a few days, huh, Mackie?"

"Yeah," Billy Mac agreed. He walked over to the creek bank and looked across to the other side. "And a couple of good hot baths didn't hurt either. Actually made my shoulder feel a lot better."

"Nice of Joseph to bring us back out tonight," Emmett said. He walked over and stood next to Billy Mac. "Wish he could've stay out here with us."

"Look at that," Billy Mac said, nodding at the creek bed. "Bone dry. Only water you can see is that little deep spot right at the bottom of this boulder."

"Unbelievable," Emmett said. "It's got to rain sooner or later."

The cicadas droned louder and then softer. Billy Mac looked up at the trees. The leaves on the sycamores were drying up and starting to fall off. *How long can this drought last? Can't remember it ever bein' this bad.*

"You know," Emmett said, "school is going to start in a few weeks. If we don't have this figured out by then, we probably never will."

"Yeah," Billy Mac said. He looked beyond the trees, into the sky. The sun had set and it was getting darker by the minute. "Emmo, are you scared?"

"I don't know, Mackie. Maybe a little. I'm not scared here where we're camping. Maybe a little apprehensive about scouting through the brush and trees on the other side, where we don't know the layout very well. You?"

"Not really scared of something happening to us or someone sneaking up on us, and we got Boomer," Billy Mac said. He looked around for the dog; Boomer was bounding in and out of the trees farther down the bank. "A little nervous about if we do find somebody that's up to something, about what we do then."

"Yeah, I know," the older boy replied. "Look, we'll take it easy. We'll be more careful and figure it out as we go. We'll agree that we won't do anything stupid. Deal?"

"Deal," Billy Mac agreed, still gazing into the sky. "Gonna be almost a full moon tonight. I say we sit tight and give it a rest for one more night."

"Me too," Emmett replied. "I'm going to build a small fire. The smoke will keep the bugs away." He turned, walked down the creek bank, and started picking up small sticks.

Billy Mac lay with his back on the sleeping bag. Boomer stretched out and braced himself next to Billy Mac's leg. Billy Mac reached down with his right hand and patted the dog.

The treetops that lined the creek were now just dark outlines against the star-filled sky. Billy Mac rolled to his left, clumsily got up—without the use of his left arm—and walked to his tent. He squatted and reached inside for his backpack and then walked back to his sleeping bag. He sat down, unzipped the pack, and pulled out his sketchpad and a pencil. He held the pencil up to the light of the sky to see if it was sharp enough and then turned a little so he could see the face of the sketch paper by the campfire light.

"Whatcha doin', Mackie?" a sleepy Emmett murmured.

"Want to see if I can sketch the trees against the sky," Billy Mac replied as he started his outline.

"You're awful good at it," Emmett said.

"Thanks, Emmo. You know Bob Follett?" Billy Mac asked without looking up.

"Yeah, sure," Emmett replied. "Works for the *Herald*. Does most of the layouts for the advertisements and pictures they use."

"Well, he's a pretty good painter—does it for a hobby, I guess," Billy Mac said. He looked up at the trees and the sky and then back down to the pad and went to work with his pencil. "Says he'll start teachin' me in the fall, how to mix paint, how to stretch the canvas and make frames. He'll try to get me started."

"Is that what you want to do when you get older, Mackie? Be an artist, a painter?" Emmett asked.

"Yeah," Billy Mac answered. "Emmo, you ever heard of TC Steele, the painter?

"Sure. Seen his name in the papers and magazines I read," the older boy replied. "Lives down in Brown County, I believe. World famous."

"Yeah," Billy Mac said. He put his pad and pencil down on his lap and looked up at the trees and sky, trying to find the right words. "Gosh. He's just . . . the best there is." He shook his head for a moment, snorted, and then picked up his pad and went back to work.

"What will you do, Emmo?" the younger boy asked. "When you get older?"

"I'd like to be a writer," Emmett replied. "Maybe a little poetry, maybe some short stories. Sell 'em to the newspapers and magazines."

"Like Riley that you're always quotin'?" Billy Mac asked.

"A person could do a lot worse," Emmett replied. "Always was partial to Riley. 'But the air's so appetizing and the landscape through the haze, of a crisp and early morning of the early Autumn days, is a picture that no painter has the coloring to mock, when the frost is on the pumpkin and the fodder's in the shock.' He sure had a way with words. Ma saw him perform some of his stuff on stage when she was a little girl. Said it was a big part of what made her want to open a theater when she grew up."

"You ever try, on your own?" Billy Mac asked. "To write stuff, I mean?"

"Yeah," Emmett said. "I keep a journal. Never told anyone that before. Not even Ma. Some of it's not too bad."

"You should go with me down to the *Herald*," Billy Mac said. "Maybe talk to the editor, Mr. Bausman. Show him what you have. He might put you to work writin' for the paper."

"Yeah!" Emmett said. "Good thinking, Mackie. I could talk to Ms. Lee about it first and see what she thinks."

"Couldn't hurt," Billy Mac said. He closed his sketch pad, stowed it and his pencil into his backpack, zipped it up, and without getting up, flung it into his tent. He lay back again, got Boomer situated with a rub on his head, and closed his eyes.

"Night, Emmo."

"Night, Mackie."

Not long after sunrise, it got too hot to sleep. Billy Mac splashed some water from the canteen on his face, shuffled through the supplies in his tent, and unwrapped a bacon biscuit sandwich. Emmett was already up and sitting on top of the boulder. Billy Mac climbed up, sat next to him in the shade, and took a bite. Suddenly, from the base of the rock, Boomer took off running for the field behind them. Billy Mac turned to see Maddie walking toward them with a smile and a wave.

Billy Mac waved at her with the biscuit in his right hand.

Emmett turned. "Hey, Maddie," he called.

Maddie walked up the rocky face and sat down next to them. "You boys look about the same. No new turn of events last night? Everyone still in one piece?"

"Yup," Billy Mac managed to say between chewing and swallowing.

"Following doctor's orders," Emmett nodded. "Quiet and peaceful night."

"It's a good thing," she said to Emmett. "Your forehead looks horrible. Starting to heal and it's turning green and red and purple."

"Starting to itch too," Emmett said, rubbing it softly.

"Want a bacon biscuit, Maddie?" Billy Mac offered. "Got one left."

"No, thanks," she answered. "I'm good."

Billy Mac thought for a minute, looked around for Boomer, and saw him off in the trees. He whistled a few times and Boomer bounded over and up the rock. Billy Mac gave him the bacon biscuit. He uncorked the canteen and poured some water into Maddie's cupped hands for the dog to drink.

"So what's the plan for today?" she asked, wiping her hands on her dress.

"Well, we know this side of the bank pretty well," Emmett said. "Let's cross over to the other side and go all the way down to where we got these the other night." He pointed at his forehead. "We can walk the tracks all the way down to the next property line and then cut in to the creek. We'll work our way back to here for lunch and then go back over and follow the bank up the other way this afternoon."

Billy Mac picked up the wrappers from the biscuits and stowed everything in his tent while Emmett put the fire out. One by one they worked their way across the tree bridge to the other side. Emmett led the way to make a path through the tall Johnson grass, and Maddie walked in front of Billy Mac. The heat was oppressive even in the early morning. The dew had long burned off, and the sweet smell of sunbaked grass filled the air. Grasshoppers skirted out of the way as Billy Mac thrashed through the growth. The trio walked down the shady side of the tracks while Boomer bounded ahead of them.

Twenty minutes later they left the tracks and cut back into the bramble to intersect the creek and work their way back. Billy Mac shot furtive glances around every now and then, a little nervous. It didn't take long to find the spot where they had been attacked. The boys reenacted a blow-by-blow narrative for Maddie and then continued on but found nothing—no signs and no clues to coincide with the pipe's message.

After lunch at their campsite, they went through the same motions, this time in the opposite direction toward town. An inconsequential morning turned into an inconsequential afternoon. At dinnertime they returned to camp.

Billy Mac sat, tired, hot, and disappointed, with Emmett and Maddie on top of the boulder. Even Boomer had had enough. He lay in a cool, shaded dirt patch by the creek bank.

Billy Mac took his shirt off and lay down with his bare back on the facing of the limestone. "Jeez! What a day."

"Yeah," Emmett answered, reaching over for Billy Mac's backpack. He opened it and pulled out the canteen. "We had to do it—had to know what was on the other side. Sure didn't help us, any though." He took another drink.

"Hey, what's that?" Maddie pointed toward the cornfield.

Billy Mac sat up and looked. He could hear someone running through the tall stalks. A second later, Joseph emerged, still running.

"Wonder what's up with him." Billy Mac waved at Joseph. As he got closer, Billy Mac could see that Joseph's ever-present smile was gone.

"Something's wrong," Emmett murmured. He corked the canteen and put it in the backpack.

Joseph reached the large boulder and bent over, panting and holding his side while trying to catch his breath. After a moment he looked up, brushed the hair out of his eyes, and wiped the sweat from his forehead with the back of his hand.

"You just aren't going to believe this," he gasped, shaking his head. He worked his way up to the top of the rock and sat down next to them.

Billy Mac, Emmett, and Maddie waited in silence.

Finally, Joseph continued. "You know how Father checks on Askuwheteau every now and then, just to make sure he's okay?"

"Yeah," Emmett replied.

"Well, I had to take some horseshoes and a harness out to the Sniders," Joseph said.

"Yeah," Emmett echoed, "so what happened?"

"Father said since I was out that way, I should stop in on Askuwheteau as it has been a few weeks since he last checked in on him." Joseph lowered his head, closed his eyes, and frowned.

"Joseph, it's okay. Tell us."

"I left the wagon down that lane a little ways from the cabin so Henry would be in the shade, and I walked the rest of the way. Askuwheteau must not have heard me coming. Before I knocked on the door, I glanced through the cabin window." He stopped and sat silent.

Maddie tilted her head and put a hand to her mouth. "Oh, my gosh, Joseph! What?"

Joseph looked up with the pain of reality in his eyes. "On the table in the cabin I saw Billy Mac's pipe!"

Chapter 26

"Jeez!" Billy Mac cried. *Then that means . . .* He looked over at Emmett.

Emmett sat back, wide-eyed. "Oh, Joseph!"

"I know," Joseph said. "I know!"

"Did you see Askuwheteau?" Maddie asked.

"Yes," Joseph answered. "I saw him through the window. He was at his sink pumping water. His back was toward me. He never saw me. I turned and hurried away. I got to the wagon and came here as fast as I could, hoping to find you all."

The wind had picked up and clouds had rolled in for the first time in many weeks. Joseph looked up at the sky and forced a smile. "The good news is it looks like we might finally get some rain later."

Billy Mac was the first to ask the obvious. "So what do we do?"

"It's going to be dark soon," Maddie said. "I'm going to have to go in. I say we leave it till tomorrow and then figure it out."

"I'm with Maddie," Joseph said. "I have to get back to town. Let's leave it until tomorrow."

Emmett was shaking his head. "We can't do that. We have to go over there. Billy Mac and I will go, and we'll come find you both in the morning and let you know if we have the pipe back or not."

"What are you going to do?" Maddie exclaimed. "Neither one of you are in any kind of shape to confront someone."

"We're not gonna cause any trouble," Billy Mac said. "We're just gonna knock on the door, tell him we know he has the pipe—but not tell him how we know—and ask for it back."

Emmett nodded in agreement. "That's all we'll do. If he gives it to us, fine. If he doesn't, fine. Either way, we'll leave and then walk back to town. I think Joseph's right. Look how the leaves are rolling their bottom sides over; rain's coming. So we'll stay in town tonight, stop by Joseph's shop in the morning, and then come back out here to let you know what happened, Maddie. Maybe in time for a good breakfast." He smiled at her.

"If you want to go now, I can drop you off at the bottom of the lane on my way back to town," Joseph said, "unless you want me to go up to the cabin with you."

"No," Billy Mac said. "You should probably stay out of it, Joseph."

"I agree," Emmett said. "He's too close of a friend to you and your father. He doesn't need to know that you're the one that told us."

"I don't have a good feeling about this," Maddie countered. "I say leave it till tomorrow. The pipe is stolen property. Billy Mac's father should go out and confront him."

"Aw, Maddie," Billy Mac argued, "it's not a big deal. He's a nice, old man. It'll be fine. Like Emmo says: If he gives it to us, fine. If he doesn't, fine. And if he doesn't, then we'll all hash it out tomorrow and come up with another plan."

Emmett stood up and nodded. "Let's go," he said, dusting off his cut-off dungarees.

The boys approached the grassy lane that led up to Askuwheteau's cabin and Joseph stopped the wagon. Billy Mac and Emmett hopped down off the bench. Joseph nodded to them. He snapped the reins and Henry started off toward town.

The two boys waved Joseph off and then turned and walked up the tree-lined lane to Askuwheteau's cabin. Billy Mac could hear thunder in the distance. He looked up and saw the wind blowing through the treetops.

"We're going to have to do this fast, Mackie," Emmett said. "Looks like it could be a pretty good storm." He started up the path.

"Yeah, okay." Billy Mac agreed and followed.

They came to the bend in the lane that curved around the cliff face. Emmett put his hand out.

"Hold up, Mackie. Let's take it slow and see if we see anything."

They inched forward. Finally, the cabin was in full sight. Nothing seemed out of the ordinary.

"What do you think, Emmo?"

Emmett looked at him and nodded once toward the cabin. Billy Mac took a deep breath, straightened up, marched with him up to the door, and knocked loudly three times.

Thunder rolled across this sky—this time closer—and the wind whipped around them. A second later the door opened and there stood the old Indian, his surprise at seeing them apparent. He hesitated and then softly said, "*Be-zone*, my young friends."

Billy Mac nodded at him. "Hello, Askuwheteau," he said awkwardly.

"Askuwheteau," Emmett said matter-of-factly, "we've come for the pipe. We know you have it."

The old man's face sank. "Yes, it is here," he finally said. He looked up at the storm clouds. A loud peal of thunder rolled by. He moved aside in the doorway. "You should come in."

Billy Mac followed Emmett and entered the rustic cabin. Inside, it implied a homey, simple life. In one corner was a cot with the blankets neatly folded. A Franklin stove and sink with a well pump were on a side wall. It was clean and free of clutter. On a table in the middle of the room was the pipe.

Askuwheteau walked over to the table and sat in one the chairs. He waved them over.

"Please, my, *neekanhuh*," he said. "Please sit. There is much you need to know."

The boys silently did as they were bid. Billy Mac pulled out a chair and sat down at the table. He looked at Askuwheteau and waited for him to speak.

Askuwheteau picked up the pipe. He turned it from side to side and then handed it to Billy Mac. "This should be returned to you, the one from whom it was taken."

"Thank you," the boy murmured, not quite sure what else to say. He put it on the table in front of him.

"Askuwheteau," Emmett said, "you said there is much we should know. Will you tell us?"

"Yes." The old man nodded. "I will tell you all that I know, but first you need to know that it was not I . . . "

The old man stopped in midsentence. He looked to the window by the front door and tilted his head, intently listening. He suddenly rose and with amazing speed went to the back wall and took his shotgun off of the pegs above the back door.

Billy Mac and Emmett both jumped up alarmed.

"What . . . ," Billy Mac started.

Askuwheteau swung around, his double-barreled shotgun pointing toward the front door as it crashed open. Billy Mac turned to look. In the doorway stood a large man, bedraggled and matted. He was an Indian, and he scowled at the three in the room.

Chapter 27

"I told you to stay out of it," the man hissed to Emmett. He looked at the pipe on the table and then at Askuwheteau. "Now, old man, I will take back what you took from me." He took a step farther into the room.

Askuwheteau thumbed back both hammers on the shotgun and the intruder stopped.

"No," Askuwheteau said. "You will leave here. You will leave and never return." Without looking at the boys, he said, "Go, my young friends, out the back there. You will find a path. Hurry!"

Billy Mac slowly reached down with his good hand—without taking his eyes off of the intruder—and grabbed the pipe. He and Emmett edged to the back door, opened it, and then ran out into the night.

Lightning flashed.

"This way," Emmett cried into the wind. "I see the path."

Billy Mac followed Emmett and they scrambled down the bluff onto the path, pushing branches out of the way and skidding down the steeper parts. Billy Mac tripped on a tree root and tumbled over and over until he stopped at the bottom of the bluff.

"Mackie!" Emmett yelled behind him. A moment later Emmett was beside him and rolled him over.

"Mackie, you okay?"

"Yeah . . . ohhh," the boy groaned. "Landed on my bad shoulder. Don't think I can—God, it hurts!"

"C'mon, Mackie." Emmett helped the boy to his feet. Lighting crashed again. The strike lit up the sky.

"Look, Mackie, we're in the creek bed. This is Pike's Creek! This is the creek that runs all the way out to Maddie's!"

A shotgun boomed and Billy Mac heard someone yell.

"Jeezus, Emmo!" Billy Mac cried.

"Look, Mackie, we can't stay here. We have to run."

"I can't run, Emmo. My shoulder is killing me."

"Okay, here's what we'll do. We're closest to Maddie's farm. You work your way down the creek and get to the farmhouse. I'll run as fast as I can and get to town and bring your pa out there."

They could hear someone at the top of the bluff cursing and working his way down the path.

"Go! Now!" Emmett yelled and pushed Billy Mac to get him started.

"Emmo, what about Askuwheteau?" Billy Mac cried. "We can't just . . ."

"We'll come back for him after I get your pa. Go! Now!"

Billy Mac turned and trotted down the dry creek bed, holding his injured arm close to his chest with his good arm. Every step shot a bolt of pain through his body. *Which way will the man go when he gets to the bottom, after me or Emmo?*

In a slow, uneven trot, Billy Mac worked his way until he came to a large fallen tree lying in the creek bed. He slipped behind the tangle of the giant root ball and squatted to catch his breath. He turned and peeked back the way he had come. He couldn't see anything. A large rain drop hit him in the forehead and then another and another.

Wind whipped the treetops back and forth and lightning flashed, the roar of thunder deafening. Billy Mac squinted and peered back down the creek bed. Far back in the shadows he saw something move and fall to the ground. "When I catch you kids," a voice yelled.

Real fear struck Billy Mac and he felt sick to his stomach. He started to run and then stopped and turned back to the fallen tree. He took the pipe and hid it deep in the tangle of roots jutting out from the base of the trunk. *I can run faster without this!* He took his free hand and cradled the elbow of his mangled arm, tucking the useless hand under the armpit of his good side. Holding it close, he turned and jogged farther down the creek bed. *Jeezus.*

Rain was coming down hard, the wind driving it sideways. Lightning crashed in all directions. Billy Mac worked his way against the torrent. Leaves and small branches ripped from the trees and pelted him, but he kept going.

Close behind, he heard someone swear. *Oh, no!* Instinctively, he hugged the side of the creek bed, trying to meld into it so he wouldn't be caught. He felt his way along. He could hear boots grinding on gravel behind him.

Billy Mac rounded a sharp bend in the creek. Lighting flashed and he realized where he was. He could see Maddie's large limestone boulder not too far ahead. The giant formation stretched all the way down to the creek bed. The rope still hung down and was blowing back and forth in the storm, right above the little ledge that stuck out. *If I can get there in time . . .*

He trotted to the rock and reached up. The rope was too high. *Got to find a way to get up higher.* He felt along the rock, working his way across. Then, on the far side, he felt a narrow opening in the facing of the limestone. *A little cave?*

He braced his feet on each side of the narrow opening and tried to inch his way higher and higher to the rope. Billy Mac slipped and fell back to the creek bottom. He tried again. He pressed the right side of his body against the opening as he braced himself with his left foot and inched his right foot a little higher. Then, pushing with his right foot, he shifted his weight to brace his injured side against the opening. White-hot pain shot through his body and he lost his footing and slid back down. *No good. I'll never make it with one arm.*

Billy Mac turned sideways and worked his way through the gap in the rock. Once inside, the space opened up a little more. Billy Mac found he could almost stand all the way up. He took a step and tripped on a rock that stuck up out of the sand. Lacking both arms to catch himself, he lost his balance and fell face first. "Argh!" he yelled, unable to stop himself from crying out.

The torso of the large man stuck through the opening, and he grabbed Billy Mac by the feet. Billy Mac thrashed and kicked to get free, but it was useless. The man slowly dragged him back to the gap in the rock. Billy Mac reached out with his good hand and grabbed hold of the rock he had tripped on. The man swore at him and he pulled, but Billy Mac clung to the half-buried rock.

All of a sudden, the rock came loose from the sand and Billy Mac was pulled to the opening of the little cave. A hand reached in, grabbed Billy Mac's wet hair, and cruelly dragged him back through the opening and into the creek bed. "Aaarrrhhhggg," he cried in pain.

The man was on him now. Billy Mac flipped over and tried to wiggle free, the pain from his shoulder unbearable. He looked up in a daze through the rain. The eyes that looked back at him burned with anger.

"Now, you," the man swore at him, "you'll give me that pipe!" He ripped through Billy Mac's pockets and inside his shirt but found nothing. "Where is it?!"

"Don't . . . have . . . it," Billy Mac grunted, trying to stay conscious.

"I swear to you, if you don't give it to me I'll—"

"Hid it. Back . . . down . . . the—"

The man grabbed Billy Mac by the front of his shirt with both hands and yanked him up. "Then you'll show me where!"

Billy Mac couldn't find his footing and slumped back down. The world was spinning.

"Get up!" The man yanked him up again.

Billy Mac heard a dog bark, another voice, and then a large thud. His attacker fell unconscious on top of him. Billy Mac opened his eyes and in a fog saw Doc Miller and Maddie standing over them. Then they faded out into blackness.

Chapter 28

Doc Miller held Billy Mac up on one side and Maddie on the other. They half carried, half walked him to the farmhouse. As they reached the door, a Model T pulled up. Billy Mac's father and Emmett jumped out.

Once inside, they placed Billy Mac on a sofa. Doc went to work on him while Emmett told the others about their visit to Askuwheteau's cabin and their flight down the bluff. Billy Mac watched Mrs. Miller flutter around the room, wringing her hands.

"He's still down there, Sheriff," Doc told Billy Mac's father as he reset Billy Mac's shoulder and worked his arm into a sling. "We left him there in the creek bed. I hit him a pretty good lick with my cane. He's likely to be out of it for a while."

"Pa." Billy Mac looked up at his father. "We got to get to Askuwheteau. We heard the shotgun go off. He might be hurt bad!"

"Or worse," Emmett said. He looked around at everyone. "We have to go now!"

"Okay," the sheriff said. "Emmett and I will go. Billy Mac will stay here with Doc. When we get back, we'll go down to the creek and get the man that's caused all this trouble."

Billy Mac slowly sat up. "No, sir. I have to go with you."

Father and son looked at each other. Finally his father consented. "Okay, son, okay." He turned and looked at Doc Miller. "You'll be okay here until we get back?"

"Sure, Sheriff," Doc Miller said. "We're boarded up pretty good. I've got my shotgun and Boomer here will let us know if anyone's creeping around outside." He reached down and rubbed the dog between the ears. "If he needs attention, bring him back here."

The front and back doors to Askuwheteau's cabin were still open, the wind and rain swinging them back and forth. The room was full of leaves and debris blowing through from the storm.

Inside, the shotgun was on one side of the table and Askuwheteau lay facedown on the other side. There was a small pool of blood under his head. They rolled him over and he groaned faintly. He had a deep gash in his forehead.

Billy Mac closed the doors to shut the storm out and turned back toward the others. Emmett cradled Askuwheteau's head. His pa found a cup and pumped some water into it. The old man opened his eyes and took a small drink of water. Billy Mac's father and Emmett helped him to the cot and covered him with blankets. Billy Mac took a wet towel from the sink and put it across his forehead.

"It is good," the old man said.

"We should take you to Doc's so he can help you," Billy Mac's father said.

"No," the old man answered, "I need to lie here. I don't believe I can do otherwise. And I need to talk with my friends here."

Billy Mac walked over. His father stood up and turned to him. "All right, I'm going back to the Millers. We'll put the man that attacked you in handcuffs, and I'll bring Doc back here." He walked out the door, and a second later, Billy Mac heard the car start off down the lane.

He and Emmett pulled chairs to the bedside.

"Don't talk now, Askuwheteau," Billy Mac said. "Just rest. We can talk later."

"I fear not, *neekanhuh,*" the old man replied. "I need to tell you what I know, now."

The boys waited for the old man as he lay with his eyes closed. Finally, he opened them and looked painfully at the boys.

"I am sorry I have not shared all with you earlier," he began. "First, you must know that I did not steal the pipe from you."

"It was the man that came here tonight?" Billy Mac asked.

"Yes," Askuwheteau answered.

"But how did he know about it?" Emmett asked. "And how did he know about the gold?"

"Because," the old man explained, "he was my son."

Chapter 29

"Your son!" Billy Mac cried. "Your son would do this to you?!"

"He *was* my son," Askuwheteau said with sadness. "He stopped being my son many years ago. When he was young we quarreled often. He had heard the stories of hidden gold and pressed me often. I told him then that I did not know the resting place of Tecumseh's gold, but he didn't believe me, for I was supposed to be the Watcher. Like me before him, he left with hate and blackness in his heart. But unlike me, he never gained in wisdom as he grew in years. His hate remained strong and he never returned. I have not known where he has been for many years—have not known, even, if he was alive.

"When you told me of seeing a person—perhaps a spirit—at the old cabin and along the tracks, you described him as being of the People. Then during your visit to me you heard and saw someone in the trees on the cliffside. Perhaps, I thought, someone was watching and listening. Thus, it made me wonder. Had my son . . . had Ahote returned? Was he watching me to see if my actions would show him the secret of the gold? I set out to look for tracks. You came to the cabin as I was readying myself to leave. Do you remember?"

"Yes," Billy Mac said. "It was after the pipe had been stolen from my home."

"Askuwheteau?" Emmett asked. "The pipe tells where the gold is buried, doesn't it?"

"I believe it to be so," Askuwheteau said. "My father entrusted the secret to the only person he knew at the time to be honorable, Doctor Miller's father, even though he was not of the People—even though he would not know the secret of the pipe."

"So your son was watching us the day of our first visit," Emmett said. "He heard us tell you that we had found the pipe and that it was at Billy Mac's house in his backpack."

"Yes," the old man said. He closed his eyes and breathed heavily. "He would have recognized the significance of the pipe," he continued. "After you left the first day, I found signs among the trees. Even after many years I could recognize the sign of my own son." He opened his eyes and looked at them both. "So I set out to track him and find him."

"On that second day that we came out," Billy Mac asked, "you were leavin' to look for him? That's why you wanted us to leave?"

"Yes," Askuwheteau answered. "When you told me the pipe had been stolen, I knew it must have been Ahote who did it. To have done a thing such as that meant he was still full of anger and greed. I was ashamed. It is why I did not reveal all to you at that time. I decided I would try, by my own hand, to recover what had been taken and to try to make things right."

"We found his campsite once," Emmett said, "on the Miller's farm next to the creek. We found his hat and some of his supplies."

"Then it was you we saw a few nights ago, very late?" Billy Mac asked. "We saw one person following another and we crossed the creek. Someone—it must have been your son—came up from behind and gave me this." He pointed at his shoulder.

"And this." Emmett rubbed his forehead.

"Yes," the old man said faintly. He closed his eyes again. "He must have known I was tracking him and he circled to get behind me. That is why he stumbled upon you. When I heard the noise of his attack on you, I hurried back. From the shadows

I watched to make sure you were not harmed too badly. When you started for Doctor Miller's home, I then picked up Ahote's sign and followed to where he camped. I waited through the night and then through the next day. I watched him and saw where he kept the pipe. He kept looking at it. I knew he was still trying to learn its secret; he was trying to remember his teachings so he could read the message. Last night an opportunity presented itself, and I snuck into his camp and took it. I planned to bring it to you and to the sheriff and tell all, but you came to me first."

Askuwheteau opened his eyes. "Now you know all there is. Forgive me for not coming to you earlier."

"We do," the boys murmured in unison.

"Askuwheteau," Billy Mac whispered, "could you read the pipe? Do you know what it says?" But there was no answer.

Emmett took the bloody towel from the old man's forehead, walked to the sink, pumped some water, and rinsed the towel out. He wrung, folded it into a long strip, and placed the cool cloth back on the wrinkled forehead.

Billy Mac heard a car come up the lane. The motor stopped and a moment later the door opened. His father, Doc Miller, and Maddie came in. Doc immediately walked over to the bedside.

"He doesn't sound good, Doc," Billy Mac said.

Doc Miller sat in Emmett's vacant chair, opened Askuwheteau's shirt, put the stethoscope in his ears, and placed the cup of the stethoscope to the old man's chest. Before long he took the stethoscope out of his ears and sat back in the chair.

"It's not good. His breathing is very, very faint," he said. "His old heart has just about had enough. There's really nothing we can do but wait."

"Dad, did you find him? Did you catch him and cuff him, the man that attacked us?" Billy Mac asked.

"No," his father answered. "We went down to the creek, and there was already three feet of water in it. I thought he might have stayed unconscious and drowned, so I combed the creek. I walked down to where a body would have gotten snagged on two old trees in the creek bed. There was nothing there. I think he survived, up and gone. We'll probably never see him again."

"He was Askuwheteau's son," Billy Mac said matter-of-factly.

Maddie gasped. "His son? Oh, my gosh!"

"I remember his son," Doc Miller murmured. "Was hoping he'd never come back to these parts. Didn't recognize him in the dark."

"He was a bad one," the sheriff nodded. "At this point he'll know that we know who he is. I'm sure he's long gone. I'll still put out a wire on him tomorrow. Maybe someone in the next county will find him."

"Oh, no!" Billy Mac cried and jumped up. "The pipe! We have to go get the pipe!"

"What do you mean?" Emmett said. "It's not at Maddie's?"

"No! I had to hide it in the creek bed so I could run faster!" Billy Mac ran to the back door and opened it. The wind had calmed down and the lightning had stopped, but the rain was heavy and pouring straight down.

"We can't, son." His father caught him by his good arm. "That creek's full up to the bank by now. It's a flash flood. We haven't had rain in so long. All the farmland around here is draining into it as fast as it can."

"I'm afraid he's right, boys," Doc said. "If you try to get into that creek now, you'll drown. It's flowing so fast you'd be pinned against rocks or logs or swept down the creek into the river. You can't fight that."

Billy Mac sat down at the table, dazed. "Then that's what happened to it. It's washed away out into the river. It's gone forever." He looked up at Emmett. "Emmo, I'm sorry. I never thought . . . "

"Mackie, it's okay," Emmett answered. He sat down in the other chair at the table. "Really, it's okay."

"He's right." Maddie put her hand on Billy Mac's shoulder. "You're both safe and most of the mystery is solved."

"*Neekanhuh*," a faint voice called. Billy Mac turned to look. Askuwheteau's eyes were barely open, but he was looking directly at Billy Mac. "Come."

Billy Mac walked over and sat down. Askuwheteau whispered something he couldn't understand. He bent over and put his ear next to the old man's mouth, and Askuwheteau whispered again. Billy Mac looked at him and nodded, and then he put his ear back down so he could hear the rest of what Askuwheteau wanted to tell him.

Billy Mac sat up and shook his head. *Unbelievable.* He looked back down at the old man and realization hit him.

"Doc!" Billy Mac called. "Doc, I think he's stopped breathin'!"

Doc and the others hurried over. Doc Miller put the stethoscope to Askuwheteau's chest. He picked up his wrist to check for a pulse. He then put his fingers on the side of the old man's neck. Finally, he said, "I'm afraid he's gone. I'm sorry." Doc sat down, placed Askuwheteau's arms across his chest, and pulled the blanket up over his face.

Maddie put her arms around Billy Mac and Emmett. They began to sob as they huddled together.

Chapter 30

Billy Mac sat with Emmett, Maddie, and Joseph on the benches in the shade outside the door of the blacksmith shop. Boomer lay in the cool of the dirt under the large sycamore.

"Can you believe this?" Billy Mac waved at the sunny sky with his good arm. "Clear as a bell. Hard to believe how nasty it was last night down in that creek bed."

"Hard to believe all that happened after I dropped you two off last night," Joseph said. "When you got the sheriff, Emmett, you should have come and gotten myself and Father. You might have needed the help!"

"Didn't have time, Joseph." Emmett shrugged. "Had to get back out there as fast as we could. Barely had time to call Doc Miller on the telephone from the sheriff's office in order to go look out for Mackie. Lucky the line was open."

"Lucky we have a telephone," Maddie said. "If it wasn't for people needing a doctor, we wouldn't even have one."

"We're sorry about Askuwheteau, Joseph," Billy Mac said softly. He kicked at the ground with his toe. "We know he was a good friend and a good man."

"We feel bad for ever suspecting him of anything," Emmett said.

"No need to be sorry, to me or to him," Joseph said. He smiled and Billy Mac nodded in silence.

"Okay," Maddie said. She turned to Billy Mac. "We need to know what Askuwheteau said to you, there at the end." She tilted her head and pushed the hair out of her eyes.

Everyone was looking at him. "Well," he said, smiling and enjoying the moment, "we know the pipe was lost in the flood, right?"

"Right," Maddie said.

"We know the first part of the clue," Billy Mac said. "'The secret lies in the mouth of,' right?"

"Right," Emmett agreed.

"Askuwheteau told me the rest of the clue," Billy Mac said. "But it still doesn't tell us exactly where to look; it's still just a clue."

"But what did he say, Mackie?!" Emmett demanded.

"First, he asked if I would take the vow that all the past Watchers have taken. I told him I would." Billy Mac paused for dramatic effect. "Then he told me the rest."

"Wait!" Maddie exclaimed. "If you took the vow, then the rest of us should too, if you're going to tell us." She looked at Emmett and Joseph. Each nodded in agreement.

Maddie leaned forward and held a hand out with the palm flat, faced down. Emmett and Joseph did the same, stacking their hands on top of Maddie's.

"Mackie?" Emmett asked.

Billy Mac reached out and put his hand on top of the others. He thought for a moment but couldn't find the words. He looked over at Emmett, silently asking. His friend understood and nodded his head.

"Askuwheteau told us that first day that each warrior actually took an oath," Emmett said. "An oath differs from a pledge in that an oath is a promise made upon something sacred or holy as witness. We don't know the words used by the original band of warriors, but we can make an oath to each other by what we hold sacred. We know the gold was to be used only to regain what the tribes of the confederacy had lost by force or broken promises. We can make an oath to the same.

To borrow the words of the preacher, we make this oath on our fear of hell and our hope of heaven." He put his other hand on top of the others.

"And upon our friendship," said Joseph. He put his other hand on top.

"So be it," added Maddie as she piled her other hand on the stack.

They looked at Billy Mac. He leaned forward so that his arm in the sling was close enough for his hand to reach out and top the others, albeit with a wince of pain. "So be it. Thanks, Emmo."

They all sat back and looked at Billy Mac.

"The secret lies in the mouth of the sleeping giant that drinks the water," he said.

Emmett furrowed his brows. "Of the sleeping giant that drinks the water? Are you sure?"

"Sure, I'm sure!" Billy Mac answered.

"But it doesn't make sense," Emmett countered.

"What if . . . ," Joseph started.

"Oh, my gosh!" Maddie interrupted. She brought both hands up to her mouth. "I know what that is! I know *where* that is!"

The three boys sat in silence looking at her. She smiled and her face lit up. She started to laugh.

"You aren't going to believe this!" she gasped between breaths.

"C'mon, Maddie!" Billy Mac cried.

"Yeah! C'mon, Maddie!" Emmett leaned over and pushed her on the shoulder.

She held both hands up to ward them off. "Okay, okay! Oh, you're not going to believe this." She got control of her laughing fit. "That large limestone cropping that I've sat on for as long as I can remember with Boomer, where we've all had picnics, that you've jumped off into the creek and climbed back up onto with that rope—that's the sleeping giant that drinks the water!"

"What?" Billy Mac quizzically countered. He cocked his head to one side. "I don't get it!"

"Listen," Maddie said. "The front of the boulder goes all the way down to the bottom of the creek."

"Right," Billy Mac said. "When I was running from Ahote, I felt my way across the face of it until I found the opening that ran up and down on the far side of it."

"You felt your way across the face of it," Maddie said, "because it *is* a face! Remember how Gramps told me when he was a boy the creek dried up and he played in the creek bed all the time? He says when the creek is dry and you're standing in the bottom looking at that giant piece of rock, it looks like a face laying on its side."

She tilted her head all the way over to one side. "There are two big indentations that look like eyes." She touched both of her eyes. "There's a flat piece that sticks out like a nose—what you two were using for a ledge when you were climbing back up the rope—and that opening Billy Mac found runs up and down for a mouth. There's a deep spot right at the bottom. It creates a gap that always has a little bit of water, so it looks like the sleeping giant is drinking. That's it!"

Billy Mac nodded. "Once I squeezed through, it opened up enough that I could almost stand up. I suppose someone could have hid something in there . . . but it was empty."

"Probably," Emmett said, "because in the last one hundred plus years, gold would have sunk in the mud and silt. Or they could have buried it in there."

"You're sure there was nothing in there, Billy Mac?" Maddie asked. "It must have been awful dark."

"Yeah," he answered and thought back to the night before. "I had just worked my way inside when I went to take a step and tripped. When I fell, my right arm went out in front of me. Then when Ahote grabbed from behind, I was kind of thrashing around. I'm pretty sure I felt all the way around the bottom of that little cave. And the lightening lit it up a little. I didn't feel or see anything that . . . "

"You tripped on what?" Joseph interrupted.

Slowly, the truth of it dawned on Billy Mac. "Oh, jeez!"

"What, Mackie?"

"I tripped on a rock—what I thought was a rock—stickin' up out of the sand." He started piecing it together. "Ahote grabbed my feet and started pullin' me out. I grabbed that rock that I'd tripped on . . . and Ahote kept pulling me."

"Yeah?" Emmett prodded him on.

"I was holdin' on to that rock for dear life with Ahote pulling on me, and then it came loose and pulled right up out of the sand. Ahote pulled me to the front of the cave and then yanked me out." He rubbed the back of his head. *Still hurts!*

He looked at the ground, shaking his head in disbelief. "That rock . . ."

"Yeah, Mackie?"

Billy Mac looked up at the others. "I'm just now thinkin'. It wasn't a rock. It was a . . . it was shaped like a brick! When it came out of the ground, I grabbed it thinkin' I could use it on Ahote. I stretched out and grabbed at it with my right hand but couldn't pick it up. It was too heavy. And it was all smooth!"

The others were as stunned by his revelation as Billy Mac was. Maddie put her hands up to mouth.

"Oh, Billy Mac!" she gasped.

"Mackie, you found it! You found the gold!" Emmett choked. He jumped up, slapped Billy Mac on the back, and danced around. "Whoo-hoo!"

Billy Mac winced from Emmett's back slap. He looked at Joseph who sat there beaming back at him.

Could it be true? What if it was? What if it wasn't? It had to be. What else could it have been? He was numb from the surreal realization. His heart pounded and he fought to catch his breath. Finally, Billy Mac found his voice.

"So what do we do?" Billy Mac said. "We gotta find out! We gotta know for sure!"

"Nothing we can do right now." Emmett walked back to his bench and shrugged. "That creek has overflowed its banks;

you saw it this morning when we got Maddie. No one's getting back down there for a few days. The current would drown you." He slapped Billy Mac on the back again. "Besides, it can't be anything else. I can't believe you did it! Whoo-hoo!" Emmett danced around again.

"Can't we dig from the top and get down to it that way?" Billy Mac asked, grasping at ideas.

"No way," Joseph said. "You can't dig through limestone. We're going to have to just wait it out till the creek calms down."

"Whatever's down there," Maddie said, "it's been there over a hundred years. It can wait a little longer. Nothing's going to happen until you both heal up, and I mean *really* heal up."

Emmett held his palm back out into the middle of them all. "Okay, hands in. We keep this to ourselves until we can get down there ourselves."

Billy Mac put his right palm on top of Emmett's. Maddie and Joseph followed.

"Good," Emmett said. "We'll—"

"Hey." Joseph cut him off. "Look what we have here."

Billy Mac looked up, expecting to see Gus and his band of boys. Instead, he saw Principal Skinner waving to them from the sidewalk. He had a smile on his face and turned to walk up to the shop.

"Hello, all," the principal said. The boys all stood up and he shook hands with them.

"Uh, hello, Mr. Skinner," Emmett said. "How are you?"

"Fine, my boy, fine," he said. "News travels fast. I was glad to know of the safe finale of last evening's events. I trust you recovered the missing—should I say stolen—tomahawk pipe?"

"Yes, sir," Billy Mac said. "But I'm afraid it was then lost in the flooding of the creek."

"Oh," the principal furrowed his eyebrows. "A pity. I should have liked to have examined it. Ah, but you are all safe and that is what counts. You know, I am on my way to the schoolhouse. I look forward to you boys, and Ms. Miller of course, being front and center when we open on the Monday after next."

Just then a green Model-T rattled by, slowed a little, and then sped off. Billy Mac was sure it was Mrs. Skinner scowling at them from behind the wheel. "Wasn't that . . . ," he started.

"Ah, yes," the principal continued. "I'm afraid it was. May I be the first to inform you of her vacating Monticello. We shan't be seeing her again. She had quite a shock this morning. It seems a small skunk found its way into her automobile to nest and was rather upset at the disturbance caused by Mrs. Skinner's desire to drive its new home about." He choked down a chuckle. "It was really quite comical, though most aromatic!"

"You mean she's—," Billy Mac started.

"Oh, sorry, sir." Emmett cut him off. "Sorry to hear that. If there's anything you need, I mean . . ." He searched for the right words.

"No matter, my boy." Principal Skinner beamed. "The town and its residents—*all* of its residents—are bound for a more tranquil existence given her departure. But I thank you for your kindness, and if you would, please express my gratitude to the more junior, albeit resolute, young men of our town. Good day!"

As he walked out of sight, the four friends busted out laughing. Billy Mac winced at the pain it caused him.

"I have a question," Joseph said as the laughter subsided. "When you get back down into that little cave and uncover the gold, what will you do with it?"

Maddie looked at Emmett who turned and looked at Billy Mac. "You're the chosen one by Askuwheteau. You're the Watcher now."

Billy Mac sat quietly for a minute. "I've thought about that a lot since Askuwheteau told me the rest of the clue last night," he said. "We'd have to do what they all promised from the beginning. It can only be used to help the People reclaim what was taken from them, what they have lost." He nodded at Joseph.

Maddie furrowed her brows. "We can't use it to buy guns and start a revolt."

"I don't mean that, Maddie," Billy Mac said. "But there are other ways."

"I think I know what he means," Emmett said. "Let me try." He thought for a moment. "They lost land, their culture, their way of life. Many of them lost their dignity from not being able to care for themselves. I think what Mackie is saying is that if we do find anything, it could be used to help them get some of that back."

"Yeah." Billy Mac nodded. "In a good, positive way."'

"Like schools?" Maddie asked.

"Maybe a cultural learning center," Joseph added.

"It could be for the People and other tribes." Emmett thought out loud. "Maybe free classes for training and skills to help find good jobs or to get into college."

"Maybe buy back some of the land that was important to them," Maddie said.

"There's lots of good things that could be done," Billy Mac said.

They sat in silence for a moment, and then Maddie said, "Well, it's about lunchtime. Ma's expecting all of us."

"Give me about five minutes," Joseph said. "I'll have Henry hooked up in no time." He stood up and walked around the corner of the shop.

Emmett nudged Billy Mac. "We did it, Mackie. We really did it!"

"Yeah." He looked up at Emmett and then Maddie. "We did. We *really* did." He finally smiled.

Maddie looked back at Billy Mac, a concerned look on her face. "You okay? How do you feel?"

Billy Mac thought for a moment. He surprised himself with his answer. "I feel . . . hungry."

"How does fried chicken sound?" she asked, her head tilted.

"Sounds good, Maddie," Billy Mac answered. "Sounds *real* good."

"Sounds great, actually," Emmett added with a smile. Maddie looked at Emmett and smiled back.

Billy Mac watched his two friends and shook his head. *Good grief.*

The End

Afterword

Four hundred million years ago, all of the earth's landmasses were part of one giant supercontinent. The area of what would become Indiana sat on the equator and was covered by a large inland sea. Coral reefs formed the base of a limestone cap that over millions of years grew to be thousands of feet thick. One hundred and eighty million years ago, this supercontinent broke up and the pieces drifted apart, taking their present-day continental shapes. Plentiful rainfall and a low elevation created a rolling landscape across the area that would become Indiana.

The last Ice Age for North America began a little over a million years ago. For tens of thousands of years, a glacier one mile thick crept south a few feet per year, grinding all that lay in its path and pushing walls of earth before it. It covered the top two-thirds of Indiana before it halted and melted. It was followed over the eons by three other glaciers, each reaching to southern Indiana. By ten thousand years ago, the last had retreated.

As each glacier advanced, they swept with them rocks, dirt, and debris. They filled in the rolling terrain and created a flat, fertile landscape across the northern two-thirds of the state. These four glaciers also formed Indiana's river systems as we know them. Where each had stopped, a ridge was formed. Multiple ridges created valleys and thus created rivers that flow northeast to the southwest, one of which is the mighty Wabash.

Just before turning south, the Wabash is joined by another river. Flowing parallel to the Wabash for 120 miles is its little brother the Tippecanoe River, draining over a million and a quarter acres and at places cutting large bluffs into its shoreline. Fed by eighty-eight lakes and countless streams, the Tippecanoe pours over five thousand cubic feet of water per second into the Wabash.

Three hundred years ago, the Miami, Wea, and Piankeshaw tribes lived in northern Indiana and along the shorelines of the Tippecanoe. Much to their protests, Potawatomies eventually migrated from the north and also settled along the Tippecanoe and Wabash Rivers. By 1790, French and English fur traders were causing unrest among Native Americans, cheating them in trade and corrupting them. The United States government established trading posts in an effort to maintain friendly relations with Native Americans and to gain their trust.

The Indiana Territory was organized in 1800. Thousands of settlers arrived each year, and when Indiana became the nineteenth state in 1816, it had a population of over sixty thousand residents. In 1834, White County was formed and Monticello—named after the home of Thomas Jefferson—was founded as the county seat, sitting high on the bluffs overlooking the Tippecanoe River.

By 1920, Monticello remained a sleepy, rural town with a population of 2,397 residents. Although electricity had been introduced several years earlier, only the stately, limestone courthouse, the shops lining the town square, and a few of the wealthier residents boasted of access. The occasional black Model-T was still the exception rather than the rule, as horse-drawn wagons dominated the town's dirt streets.

The main characters in this story are fictitious. They were not developed to portray any real persons, living or dead. The newspaper article in the Prologue, however, is real. Likewise, the back story of Tecumseh and his brother Tenskwatawa, the Prophet, are portrayed as accurately as possible. I've also portrayed 1924 Monticello, Indiana, as accurately as possible. The Carnegie library on the bluff of the Tippecanoe River mentioned in the story still stands—a beautiful building that today houses the White County Historical Society and Museum. It is a wondrous place. I would have liked to include more details of the town during that time period—the building of the Norway and Oakdale Dams, adverts from the *Herald* professing White's Cream Vermifuge as a remedy for a child stricken with worms, Vaudevillian handbills and adverts from the Strand Theater—but those are for another story at another time.

As referenced in the story, James Whitcomb Riley (October 7, 1849-July 22, 1916) was an American writer, poet, and best-selling author. He was born in Greenfield, Indiana, and made Indianapolis his home during his adult years. During his lifetime he was known as the Hoosier poet and the children's poet for his dialect works and his children's poetry. His famous works include "Little Orphant Annie" and "The Raggedy Man." *(Source, The Best of James Whitcomb Riley)*

Also referenced in the story, Theodore Clement Steele (September 11, 1847-July 24, 1926) was an American Impressionist painter known for his Indiana landscapes. Steele was an innovator and leader in American Midwest painting and is considered to be the most important of Indiana's Hoosier Group painters. In addition to painting, Steele served on art juries that selected entries for national and international exhibitions, including the Universal Exposition (1900) in Paris, France, and the Louisiana Purchase Exposition (1904) in Saint Louis, Missouri. *(Source, The House of the Singing Winds: The Life and Work of T. C. Steele)*

Made in the USA
Columbia, SC
04 February 2021

32330157R00105